Moodie's Tale

Canadian Cataloguing in Publication Data

Wright, Eric
Moodie's Tale

ISBN 1-55013-571-6

I. Title.

PS8595.R58M66 1994   C813'.54   C94-931239-8
PR9199.3.W75M66 1994

Key Porter Books Limited
70 The Esplanade
Toronto, Ontario
Canada M5E 1R2

The publisher gratefully acknowledges the assistance of the Department
of Communications, the Canada Council and the Ontario Arts Council.

Design: Tania Craan
Typeset in Monotype Perpetua 13/15 by Indelible Ink

Printed and bound in Canada

94 95 96 97 98 99 6 5 4 3 2

Moodie's Tale

Eric Wright

KEY PORTER·BOOKS

CONTENTS

PROLOGUE

THE LETTER FROM the Council for the Arts read, in part, *It was not easy for the committee to refuse such an excellent application, one which would certainly have found favour at another time. But, to be candid, it was such a good year for Romantic poetry that, conversely, it was a bad season for the many, many good candidates who wished to study in such a narrow field. Of necessity, the Council had to take into account our duty to avoid creating a glut of specialists down the road. Thus it is with much regret that I am writing to tell you . . .*

William dropped the letter into the wastebasket and took down his atlas to look at the map of Canada.

He had just finished a very pleasant two years at Simcoe University as a graduate student straight from Cambridge, England, and he wanted very much to stay, or, at any rate, not to have to go home yet.

Whenever people asked him why he had come to Canada he told them truthfully that it was because he had been offered a fellowship at Simcoe. But Simcoe had been only one of a number of possibilities at the time; the real reason he had wanted to come was a romantic image he had carried with him since he was six or seven, a picture compounded of Mounties, trappers, the Rocky mountains, waving wheatfields, Indians, and a huge river which one navigated by canoe in a fur hat. He had seen nothing like this so far, though many of the people he had met had testified it was still there, somewhere, and he wanted to know about it. If he had saved any money, now would have been a good time to satisfy his curiosity, but he was penniless. Now his teaching fellowship had not been renewed, and the Council for the Arts had been his last hope. Now he was going to have to get a job, and lacking marketable skills of any kind, it would have to be some kind of teaching. Next day he went to see Professor Jarvis.

As head of one of the larger graduate English programs in the country, Jarvis was regularly consulted by colleagues at other universities looking for teachers, and by the students Simcoe had finished with who were looking for jobs. He motioned William to a chair and stood himself behind his desk, directly under a huge portrait of Samuel Taylor Coleridge, thus seeming to turn the poet into an ancestor. There began a three-way conversation between Jarvis, William, and the secretary, who sat typing in an outer office with the door open.

"Miss Anderson," Jarvis bawled. "What is left on the file?"

"Micmac, Van Horne, and the one in Flin Flon," the secretary shouted back.

"Micmac, Van Horne, and the one in Flin Flon," Jarvis translated to Moodie. He looked at William, puzzled. "I thought we sent Mr. Chan to Flin Flon yesterday," he shouted through the doorway.

"He wouldn't go. He said he'd rather go back to the Philippines."

Jarvis looked at William for some seconds, measuring him. "Micmac, I think," he said.

"No, no," Miss Anderson shouted. "I thought that lad from Manitoba would be better for Micmac. Mr. Rodgers."

William brightened. Micmac was at the bottom of the list of desirable colleges, worse than third-rate. A small Anglican college on the banks of the St. John River, it was the only college in Canada that had remained the same size since the thirties. Everyone knew about Micmac. It came to him then that Dr. Jarvis had not the faintest idea who he was in spite of the fact that William had taken his course. He realized, simultaneously, that he had Miss Anderson to thank for elevating him at least above the level of "suitable for Micmac." She it was who ran the system at this level. He was glad he had bought her a little cactus for her desk.

"Why don't you take your doctorate?" Jarvis said, suddenly.

"Here, sir?" William's hopes rose; perhaps Jarvis had a fellowship left over after all.

"No, no. Not *here*. Wisconsin, somewhere like that."

"I'd need some money, sir."

"Yes, of course you would," Jarvis agreed.

"Besides, I've been a university student for five years and I want to see if I can teach before I go any further."

"Yes?" Jarvis pulled a hair out of his nose, making his eyes water. William felt him growing bored.

Miss Anderson shouted through the door. "Your sister phoned to remind you to get your hair cut before you come home."

Jarvis felt the fresh grey stubble on the back of his neck. "I got it cut this morning. What is this Flin Flon thing, Miss Anderson?"

A chair scraped and she walked in, talking as she approached. "I told you all about it yesterday. Someone has opened a junior college there. The notepaper just says Flin Flon College. They want a professor of English and French to teach English to the French and vice versa. It says an interest in hockey is an advantage. Ice hockey, I think they mean."

Jarvis raised his eyebrows at William invitingly.

"I can't speak French," William said.

Jarvis took the file from his secretary. "Van Horne it is, then. Let's see. 'The W.C. Van Horne Institute requires an instructor in English immediately. Salary to be negotiated.' There you are. Name your own price." He gave the file back to his secretary and moved towards the door. "Learn the trade and come back to us when you feel the need for the cloisters again." His last words floated back from beyond the outer door.

Miss Anderson said, "Not a real university, of course, but it's just across the park."

William left.

I
The Van Horne Institute
of the Technological Arts

i. The New Learning

THE W.C. VAN Horne Institute had a higher place than Micmac on Jarvis's list only because it paid more money. Academically the two institutions pursued very different objectives. Micmac, though it had been left behind by the age, was a historic seat of learning, one of the first centres of culture in the New World. Van Horne, on the other hand, sucked virtue from a stance of newness, boasting that it was taking care of the needs of "today's students in tomorrow's society."

It had been invented by the Ministry to take care of the enormous flood of students after the Second World War, but in the short time of its existence it had changed its name twice and the names of some of its buildings several times. It began life as the Shaftsbury Technical College, so named on the suggestion of a learned deputy minister. Then, after a change of government and the arrival of a new minister who saw an opportunity, a charter was proposed and the college was renamed after the new minister's uncle, a leading member of the party and a man of the same name as the minister. The minister thought the title "Technical College" not striking enough for his purpose, and asked for a new one. "Polytechnic" sounded too European. "Technical University" was thought a bit grand for the offering of courses in watch-repairing. Someone suggested "Technicalogical Institute" and it nearly slipped through. Finally the minister agreed to "The Ed Flint Technicon." Five years and another election later and another new minister proposed that such an important addition to the educational scene ought to be above politics, and as for "Technicon" it sounded like a slide show, so his civil servants put together the name of one of Canada'a greatest technologists with a two-word description of the college's aspirations and they arrived at "The W.C. Van Horne Institute of the Technological Arts."

The institute comprised three buildings. The original main building, a three-storey grey concrete structure occupying one side of a small city block, had once been a flourishing Bible college, but the sect had dwindled and the survivors were happy to trade it to the government for the right to grant degrees and a small historic house that the government did not know what to do with. The two other buildings were the institute's first residence — a six-bedroomed house, formerly used as a home for destitute senior citizens — and the old Wandlyn Drug Company warehouse, donated to the college when the drug company moved to the suburbs. This building housed the machine shop on the ground floor and six small classrooms in a kind of gallery under the roof. These three buildings acquired, one after the other, all the names the college discarded: the "Shaftsbury Building," the "Ed Flint Building," the "Conklin Building," and the "Clyde Dimmesdale Annexe," depending on who was in power. These changes happened quickly and regularly enough so that even the students were never sure in the early days which name was attached to which building, and the graduates required other, more permanent names, to be able to reminisce comfortably. Thus the buildings were soon known by everyone as the "Bible College," the "Old Folks' Home," and the "Drug Mart." One day a sophisticated president with a taste for inverted snobbery would see the cachet in these nicknames and cause them to be permanent, but this was a long way in the future, when "Van Horne," as everyone would refer to it, would cover twenty-five blocks of the city's downtown and be as hard to get into as M.I.T.

The Department of Communication Arts was housed in the Bible School, and here, the next day, William came for an interview with the chairman of the department.

Scyld Dunvegan was a big man wearing a navy blue blazer and striped tie, a shirt with buttons on the collar, grey flannel trousers, and loafers. He looked like a sports announcer.

"Moody? Only in name, I hope. You'll need all your spirits here." Dunvegan stood up, took off his jacket, and unzipped his trousers. He carefully rearranged his shirt-tails and zipped himself together again. He examined his jacket for specks and put it back on, then lowered himself carefully into his chair, looked at himself in a little mirror on his desk, placed his forearms together, and waited.

"No," William said. "Moodie, as in Susanna."

"I'm not with you."

"Susanna Moodie. *Roughing It in the Bush.*"

Dunvegan stared at him, saying nothing.

"'I,' 'E,'" William said. "She spelt it like me. 'I,' 'E.'"

Dunvegan said, "Let's get on, shall we? We need a versatile man, prepared to teach our students something useful. Someone who can provide what they need. Real hands-on know-how. Can you do that?"

"What sort of thing would that be?"

"English. You *are* the guy that Jarvis sent?"

"Yes. I mean what kind? Milton? Modern Drama? Canadian Literature?"

"You don't know much about us, do you?" Dunvegan lined up a piece of paper with the edge of his blotter. "Here we are. Here's the timetable I have to fill. Two sections of Business Correspondence, two sections of Public Speaking, two sections of Grammar, and one of Remedial English to bring a few of them up to our level. How does that sound?"

"No literature?"

"Not for a new man. The senior students get a course, 'Stories for Today,' and the girls in dressmaking get a course in great fairy stories, which we teach with a psychological approach. After a few years, you might offer one of your own, if we get a demand. What's your field — this Susanna Moodie woman?"

"I was researching a thesis on the insect imagery of Keats's juvenilia."

"Yeah? Then maybe a little course on nature poems, something like that? We'll have to see. Nothing too specialized." Dunvegan looked at his watch. "Let me introduce you to your colleagues."

"You mean I'm hired?"

"I hope so. The director has the final say. You'll meet him this afternoon."

"I doubt if he had any other applicants, and besides, he wants to go sailing this afternoon."

The speaker was Geoffrey Spindle, a man of about fifty, to whom William had expressed his surprise at the ease of his interview with Dunvegan. After Dunvegan had made the introductions, the Department of Communication Arts had invited him to lunch. They were all there except Dunvegan, sitting around a table in the O'Kum Inn, eating the business-man's special. Spindle continued: "Our chairman sails; rides; fishes; hunts; runs; plays squash, tennis, and golf; and he watches football, hockey, and basketball on television. He is a sport." Spindle gave no hint of his attitude to this catalogue as he carefully arranged a bacon, lettuce, and tomato sandwich in his fingers so that he could eat it neatly.

"Geoffrey's a cynic," Mordecai Redburn said. He was a small erect man with bright grey hair and a youthful face, like someone who has suffered a shock. Apart from his hair, his most arresting feature was his eyes, which were black and brilliant. The total effect was of a simple-minded boy in a grey fright wig.

Jack Bodger chimed in, a small, very fat man with a bald head and a closely shaven fringe. He was dressed in the two halves of very similar suits, a khaki shirt, and a club tie. "Never mind Geoff," he said. "Geoff's got no time for anybody. I noticed in your application you've just come from studying. Literature, was it? We should teach more of it here, if you ask me, never mind all this marking. I like literature." He looked around the table for approval.

Maisie Clipsham, the fourth and last member of the department, was an attractive lady of about thirty who looked powerfully clean. Her hair shone, as did her face and ears. Her hands looked rawly scrubbed for surgery. Her costume consisted of pale ironed cloths that seemed to have been put on five minutes before. She ate in a manner designed to avoid contact with the food until it disappeared in small bites down her throat. She said, "Teach them something you can mark without reading. Something out of ten. First thing I learned here. Never mind Chaucer. Drill them. Give them shit," she ended, mysteriously.

William suspected that the coarseness was supposed to counteract the physical impression of clinical sterility.

"I was thinking more of one of those hobbit books," Bodger said. "Not Chaucer."

Spindle stopped eating and turned slowly to confront Bodger. "Have you read them?" he asked, in a tone offensive enough to have wounded the sensibility of a prison guard.

"No, but they're kids' books, aren't they? They're all the rage."

"The shortest one is about four hundred pages long," Spindle said.

"What are they about?"

"Elves."

Redburn spoke up. "It takes me about three weeks to get through a short story. I can only get through three or four a term, and even then I've got a lot of notes left over. I like to have them read the stories aloud, too. It all takes time, and there's a lot of other stuff to get through. I spend the whole of the last month of term on 'The Letter of Application.'"

"We have to do our best for these lads," Bodger said. He drew on his pipe like an old salt in a nineteenth-century painting. "Prepare them for life."

"'Tales of the North' with questions at the back?" Maisie asked, without sarcasm, more to keep the conversation going.

"Poetry," Spindle said. No one said anything, so he said it again. "Poetry. Shakespeare's sonnets. Make them learn one a week, by heart. When they leave they'll know seventy sonnets and nothing else. Like a priesthood. The only people in Canada who know what they know. Prepare them for tomorrow: 'A Van Horne graduate is never out of date,'" he finished, intoning.

"Geoff's not serious," Bodger explained to William. "Seriously, Geoff, some of the older poems might be all right. 'The

Highwayman Came Riding,' say. None of these haycues, though."

On they went. William listened and nodded and smiled, saying little, recognizing that they were putting on a performance for his benefit, summarizing themselves out of bits of old conversations.

In the afternoon he met the Director of Humane Studies, a small, bony man with a shaven head who sat behind his desk, smoking and watching him. After several minutes the director said, "If you plan to stay you ought to sit down," and barked with laughter.

William sat, and for a very long time, perhaps three minutes, nothing happened as the director continued to stare at him through the smoke. "You married?" the director asked suddenly.

"No." William wondered if that made him more or less eligible.

There was another long pause, then the director left the office for a quarter of an hour. When he returned, he looked closely at William and gave him a form to fill out. Once again he left William alone as he listed his personal details. The form took two minutes to complete, and after waiting another half-hour William went in search of the director.

"I haven't forgotten you," the director snapped when William found him removing pins from a notice board in the corridor. William went back into the office and waited a further quarter of an hour.

The director returned and looked at him steadily as he closed the door behind him, pulled out his chair, and sat down. "You ever taught before? What do you know best?" he asked.

"I tutored classes in eighteenth-century poetry at the university. My best paper at Cambridge was on the English Moralists."

The director looked at him sideways, grinning, as if he appreciated a good liar when he met one. He got up and strolled about the room until he reached the door and darted through it. He returned after ten minutes. "Won't be long," he said, and disappeared for a further fifteen minutes. This time when he returned, he sat at his desk and smiled at William.

"I'm Clem Stokes," he said. "Director of Humane Studies. We farted around with my title for a long time. 'Director of Human Studies' made the other guys sound inhuman. 'Director of Humanistics' didn't sound right. 'Director of Humanities' — too artsy. Besides I'm responsible for Related Studies, too. That's my other department, includes everything we do except communications and a course in life insurance, you know, how much you ought to have when you get married. Guy who teaches that said it was more of a social science. So it's Humane Studies. We look after the aesthetics and language skills areas and leave the rest to Industrial Arts and Commercial Science. That make sense?"

William nodded, too interested in the contrast between the formerly silent Stokes and the man who was now chattering away at top speed to take in what he was saying.

The director continued. "All you have to do is teach them how to spell and all about the good life. Penmanship and Plato. In other words, keep them busy, keep them quiet, and keep your hands off the girls, and the boys." He looked hard at William. "And keep good time. The four K's. Thirsty?" He looked at the clock.

"No."

"Good. You're in. But you don't get your first cheque for six weeks in case you go over the wall." The director stood up.

They shook hands and William walked out to Old Street, to the nearest bar.

"He was trying to find out if you are an alcoholic," Geoffrey Spindle said, later that afternoon, when William went to the department to collect his timetable. "He has a theory about hiring new faculty. Make the interview last for two hours. Then, if the candidate is a lush, he will start to shake. If he isn't a lush, then he can probably teach as well as anyone. Clem is from Alberta. The truth is that Van Horne in its early days did attract one or two from the bottom of the ladder who fell off when they got here."

"Early days? It's only ten years old now."

"That's a cycle of Cathay for Van Horne."

ii. A Man in the Ranks

CLASSES DID NOT begin until Monday, but William was ordered to report the following morning to a classroom in the Bible School where, along with ten or twelve other new teachers, he was to take a two-day course to "orientate" him into the unique world of Van Horne.

Clem Stokes, the Director of Humane Studies, was in charge. He was being assisted by half-a-dozen colleagues.

"Right," Stokes shouted, when they were all assembled. "Tell us who you are. You start us off." He pointed to an elderly man with a silver beard. "Who are you?"

The bearded man whispered his name.

"You hear that, Fred?" Stokes shouted over the head of the bearded man.

From the rear of the room, one of Stokes's colleagues shouted back, "Didn't catch it, Clem."

"Have to do better than that, then," Stokes said, and waited. The bearded man failed to understand at first, then looked around in the silence, stood up and bellowed, "Harold Stacey," turned dark red, and sat down again.

"Good on you, Harold," Stokes said. "Next?"

One by one, the example of Stacey before them, the new teachers stood up and shouted their names: a middle-aged man from Yorkshire, four or five variously accented men from central or eastern Europe, an old Irishman, a blonde Canadian girl, a bitter-looking woman in her forties who reeked of whisky and was gone the next day, and a small, plump man who fell asleep and had to be woken up to give his name.

"Right," Stokes said when the last shouted name died down. "I want all of you out in front. Yes, you, too, Harold. Right, line up in a row. Wake that guy up, would you? That's it, all in a line."

Stokes walked to the centre of the room and turned to face the line-up, like someone preparing to give the order to march. "Now repeat after me: 'I know a man in the ranks.' Go on, 'I know a man in the ranks.'"

It took them a minute to realize what Stokes wanted, then a mumble like the sound of a small insurrection ran up and down the line and died.

"Try it again, after three. One, two, three: 'I know a man in the ranks.'"

This time they mumbled it more or less together, making a sound like a communal prayer. Stokes nodded.

"Who's going to stay in the ranks."

"Who's going to stay in the ranks," they intoned.

"Why?" Stokes asked.

"Why?" they prayed.

"Because he *hasn't* the a*bili*ty to *get things done*."

They ended the lesson and waited. "Once more," Stokes said, and they went through it again. Now they had it by heart.

"Now. This time like this: 'I KNOW A MAN IN THE RANKS,'" Stokes bawled, tripling the volume and raising his right arm on the "I."

When they had repeated it with the gesture, he shouted "WHO'S GOING TO *STAY* IN THE RANKS." Decisive down-pointing gesture on "stay."

They pointed decisively.

He led them on. "WHY?" Arms outstretched in appeal.

"WHY?" they pleaded.

"I'LL TELL YOU WHY." Gesture with right hand out, palm facing the audience.

"I'LL TELL YOU WHY," they insisted.

"Because he HASN'T the ABILITY to GET THINGS DONE." Punching the right hand into the left palm to emphasize every major word.

Watching each other to keep in step, they beat out the line.

"Once more now," Stokes said.

Harold Stacey, the elderly silver-haired man, put up his hand. "Why are you making us do this?"

Stokes said, "You're embarrassed, right, Harold?"

"Deeply."

"Don't be embarrassed. The welding students will dance on your head if they see that. Okay. Once more then."

Stacey said, "I can't do this." He looked for support along the row, but no one else broke ranks. "I can't do this," he repeated, and left the room.

Stokes was unperturbed. "One down, nine to go," he said as the door closed. "Once more, then."

Nine trainee teachers chanted the jingle with gestures. The elderly Irishman, standing next to William, said to him, "We don't do anything like this back home, as far as I've heard tell, but you expect things to be a bit different out here, don't you?"

"Now," Stokes said. "We are going to have a little competition. I'm going to divide you into threes. Each group will do it together, and the winners will compete in the grand finale."

William was in the first group. The Irishman was on his left. The pretty Canadian girl was on his right.

"Loudest wins," Stokes said. "On your marks. Go."

The Irishman raised a knee, then flicked himself upwards like a salmon leaping, turned black, and began to bellow. The pretty girl cut through his noise with a voice like a referee's whistle. William threw himself into the competition, sounding to himself like someone pleading for his life to a stone-deaf assassin, but between these two he was invisible and silent. The noise from the other two died down, and they were voted co-winners. William wondered if he had lost his job. Dr. Stokes patted him on the shoulder. "You're the shy type, too, but you're trying," he said. "Practise it on your own."

The competition proceeded, but nobody could match the first pair of winners, who moved smoothly through to emerge still tied at the end. The Irishman was certainly the noisiest, but the girl, it was felt, could command just as much attention from a class of students, which was the point.

During a break, the Irishman confessed to William that he, too, felt like an arsehole shouting like that, but he had a wife and four children, and he needed the job.

After lunch they were given problems, or rather one problem with three parts. They were asked, collectively, to comment on a situation in which two students get into a fist-fight (a) in the classroom, (b) in the corridor, and (c) outside the institute. What was the teacher's role in each case? William guessed correctly that there would be plenty of volunteers to respond, and he put on an interested face and day-dreamed behind it while the discussion went on. When the trainees had finished, each of the old hands who had been sitting in the back of the room gave a brief talk on his experiences teaching at Van Horne. At the end of each talk, the little fat man opened an eye and looked at William, then closed it and went back to sleep. But when Stokes made his final remarks the man anticipated the end by several seconds, opened both eyes, and was first out of the room.

On Friday morning they got a lecture on the history of education. The lecturer was a member of Van Horne's Commercial Science division who had got the subject up for the occasion.

"The history of education really begins with the Christians," he began. "Before the Christians there were just the pagans, and we all know about the pagans — 'All play-and-you-know-what and no work.'" He winked at William.

"That would be Plato, would it, Calvin?" Clem Stokes called out encouragingly.

"Basically, Clem. Yes, basically Plato. Others, too, though." He searched his mind. "Aristotle, Homer . . . , all those."

After him came the president, Dr. Gravely Cunningham. He wore an academic gown and spoke slowly with a slight tremor. He began with a long pause, holding the lectern and looking around the room, his head bobbing gently as if on a spring.

"Go to hell," he said suddenly. There was a long pause, measured by the bobbing of his head. The room was silent, attentive.

"I see I've got your attention," Cunningham said. "Without that, I'd be dead. You'll be dead, too, if you don't get their attention. The students at Van Horne need to be *grabbed*. Grab them. My name is Gravely Cunningham. Welcome to Van Horne." He walked out. The training session had ended.

"He calls them his 'little shockers,'" Spindle said. "He got the idea at a conference."

They were sitting after lunch in the department office, actually a large space where two corridors met, roughly furnished with some tables and chairs. In the angle of the corridors, a sheet of plywood had been erected to make an office for Dunvegan, the chairman. William had returned to the office hoping to find Spindle, who spent most of his spare hours at his desk and seemed to have plenty of time to chat. He had taken to William and required very little prodding to tell him about life at Van Horne.

They moved on to the problem of teaching, which was beginning to concern William. He suspected his experience conducting seminars would be of little use here.

"If you're here for a week you develop a theory," Spindle said. "You will know by Monday evening if you are going to survive. There are people who stay in teaching who never really did survive their first day, of course. The profession is full of cripples, although perhaps they are simply more obvious, more painful to look at, as it were, than the failures in other professions."

"What's your theory, Geoffrey?"

"I translate," Spindle said. "I discovered very early that most students cannot understand the written word as it comes to them in imaginative literature, and I also discovered that they like to be involved and active, so I teach them as I was taught Latin. I get them to read aloud and I translate. To keep them on their toes, I pick them at random — they are supposed to have prepared the text, of course — and make them write out any words they don't know. Last year I tried a story by Somerset Maugham, but that was *too* wordy. They found his sentence rhythms alien, too. We spent a week on a page. This year I have chosen something so simply written that even the lads studying Municipal Landscaping will be able to sight-read it. Hemingway."

"The students are that bad?"

"They are not much worse here than anywhere else. I've taught in a university, and the situation was not so different. Anything written before 1945 presented real difficulties, especially for students in medicine and architecture. But in the major universities you can ignore the problem by lecturing at them six hundred at a time, and getting graduate students to mark their essays, essays which are often written by professionals for a fee, so they are usually quite readable. Then if there is no exam, which happens in some of the social sciences, I believe, the ugly facts need never be faced. Here, you are confronted with them because the rooms will only hold thirty students, so you have to try to teach them. I suspect that the good students teach themselves, and the rest learn what we require of them in order to pass the examinations. After all, our real job is to sort them and grade them to save potential employers the bother. For that, the pay is quite good."

"Why did you come here?"

"I'm a specialist in Anglo-Saxon and we're a dying breed, the next to go after the classicists. The universities wouldn't have me in case I tried to offer a course in my specialty, and I was thrown on the market, as they say in Retail Merchandising. So I concealed my speciality and got a job here, teaching English. Fortunately I'm not married. It could be worse. I could have been forced to go to library school, like so many of my friends."

"What about the other people? How did they get here? Mordecai, for instance."

"Redburn's graduate speciality is the Tractarian Movement. He was studying theology and got bored with it, so he switched to English and Nineteenth-Century Thought, and having read the Bible gave him a head start. He has a brilliant degree and ought to have had a lot of offers. But he looks

funny, have you noticed? He could never survive the inter-
views, until he was interviewed by Clem Stokes."

"What's his theory of teaching?"

"The group approach. He picked it up from teaching
Sunday school. Mordecai divides them up into small discussion
groups, whatever the subject, and he walks about listening
while they discuss the topic among themselves. Then, when the
class is almost over, he has the group leaders report, verbally,
and bring back a written version to the next class. Then, for
the next class, he divides them up so they can discuss the
reports. It goes on endlessly."

"What does Jack Bodger do?"

"He uses psychology, he says. When Bodger first read the
text that he uses in English for Advertisers he was bowled over
by its subtlety. He spends all his time with his students getting
them to sell themselves, in prose, that is."

"And Miss Clipsham?"

"Ah, yes, Maisie. Have you noticed how clean she is? Bodger
says you could eat your dinner off her, and he would probably
like to. With Maisie the word is 'drill.' Do the exercises on
page twenty, and when you've finished do the ones on page
twenty-one. Every day, ten minutes on the comma splice,
perhaps, then forty minutes of drill. It has no effect on their
syntax, of course, and she doesn't claim that it does, but they
do know those exercises."

"Does Dunvegan teach?"

"Oral Communication only."

"Public speaking?"

"Private speaking, really. How to conduct yourself in what
he calls a one-on-one situation. How to talk to the boss. How
to fire an employee so that he likes it. How to talk on the
telephone. The spoken arts, generally. And now that's enough

gossip. Let me find you the texts you'll need and you can spend the weekend studying. That should give you enough for a semester."

William understood that Spindle had just performed for his benefit, given his impersonation of the once brilliant scholar who has drifted to the bottom of his profession, a role borrowed from so many plays about English public school life. But, whereas the chief effect of the originals that Spindle drew on was pathos, Spindle excited no such response because he had so obviously made himself at home, literally and spiritually, behind his desk in the Communication Arts department at Van Horne.

iii. Entering the Lists

THE BUSINESS CORRESPONDENCE text took him an hour to read, and he estimated that it contained enough material, stretched out, for three classes. Bodger had told him that the students used it for two years. Evidently there was a difference between reading and teaching. The Grammar text was more promising. It contained the material for a dozen spelling bees and a lot else besides, like exercises on "Ten Uses of the Comma" and "Making the Parts Agree." There was no text for Public Speaking, so William had to spend Sunday afternoon on a tour of the bookshops that were open, looking for self-help books on the subject. Like most new teachers, William's chief fear was that he would have nothing to say, and he spent the rest of the weekend in a funk, searching restlessy through the Business Correspondence text for anything he had missed, trying to write up his opening remarks in each subject.

At nine o'clock on Monday morning he met his first class in Business Correspondence. There were twenty-five students waiting for him. He introduced himself, wrote his name and the name of the text on the blackboard, and panicked. Beyond reading aloud from the text he could think of nothing else to do. He stared at a student with thick glasses in the front row who peered back at him, pencil at the ready. Finally, he remembered what he had planned.

"Right," he shouted. "First of all, I want to get some idea of the problem. You are going to write a letter to your local supermarket complaining about the quality of a product you have recently purchased." He looked down at the front row.

The student with the thick glasses peered back at him, terrified. "Me?"

"All of you."

There was a silence. "All of us *what*, sir?" the same student asked.

"Write a letter."

"Who to?"

"Your local supermarket."

"What about?"

"Complaining about something you've bought."

"Why? What's wrong with it?"

"I don't know. Invent something."

A student at the back turned to a friend. "What the fuck's he talking about, Joe?"

"Christ knows."

Starting with these two, then in a widening circle, most of the students put down their pencils in disgust and turned to each other for elucidation. "All of us? Does he mean all of us? All write one letter? How will that work? You mean we all write different letters? All of us?"

William shouted through the hubbub, "Each of you take a piece of paper and begin."

A student at the back asked, "What is this product, sir?"

"Whatever you like."

"Will meat do?"

"Certainly. Don't all do meat, though."

"We can make up anything we like?"

"That's right. Off you go."

"And we can say what's wrong with it?"

"YES! It may be broken, or spoiled, or mislabelled, or . . ."

"Rotten?"

"Yes, if you like."

"How about if it doesn't fit, sir. Something that's supposed to fit."

"That's the idea. Now, write a letter saying you are unhappy and why, and what you think they should do about it."

"This the same letter?"

"YES! Go on, get on with it."

"Now, sir?"

"Yes, yes. Now." William felt as if he were ordering them to pick their way across the ice-floes in a fast-moving river. He started to walk briskly up and down the aisles.

Gradually they began. First they assembled paper and writing instruments. Then they searched around to make sure they were near someone with a dictionary. After ten minutes, one student put up his hand. "Do you want us to write the 'Dear Sir' stuff, and do the envelope? I don't have any envelopes with me."

"Just write the letter as you think it ought to be written and don't worry about the envelope."

At the end of the forty minutes, very few had finished, and when William started to gather their papers in, several protested. "All right," William said. "Keep it until Wednesday and bring it with you to class."

"Could we hand it in now if we've finished?"

"Yes. Perhaps you should all hand it in, however far you've got. Yes. All of you. Whatever you've done. Hand it in."

"Shall we put our name on it, sir?"

"Put your name on your paper before you hand it in," William bawled. "And don't ask me where. Anywhere."

Public Speaking was next. This turned out to be easy. He divided the class into pairs and told them to be ready to debate one of a list of resolutions he had prepared. He told them to speak clearly and persuasively. They would be allowed five minutes each and the class would vote a winner. He, William, would offer further criticism by way of a mark.

The first topic was "Prostitution Should Be Legalized." William had intended it to be an occasion for wit. The opening speaker, a "mature student" in his early forties, explained in detail what it felt like to need the services of a prostitute and be unable to find one in a strange town. His opponent was Vietnamese, a Mr. Ng. He had listened carefully to William, noting particularly the advice to be persuasive. When his turn came he began on a very angry note. "My opponent is ridiculous," he screamed, black in the face. "I have never heard such ridiculous words." He yelled abuse at his opponent for the full five minutes, making no reference whatever to the topic, looked at his watch and sat down. The class listened attentively, then fell into arguments among themselves as to the relative merits of the two speakers. The ballot was secret and William pronounced the result a tie, declining to give a deciding vote and giving each of the speakers six-and-a-half out of ten. He then chatted to the class, finding it easy to extemporize by using the examples of the two speeches they had heard, and was astonished to hear the bell ring for the end of the class.

Grammar was, if anything, easier. The text, *Grammar for Grownups*, was accompanied by a set of exercises, and, with a minimum of exposition, William was able to use the whole time in identifying nouns. Each student took one line of text and searched in turn for nouns. As each student announced the nouns he had found, the others tried to identify his errors and omissions. Then William gave them the correct answers. There was enough in the grammar text for several years.

Lunch came and with it the discovery that William was the only one teaching. The others had been collecting names, discussing course outlines, and doing other jobs of an introductory nature. Jack Bodger said, "You can push these kids too hard, you know. I like to take it easy with them for the first couple of weeks."

In the afternoon, William repeated the sequence of classes to three different groups. At the end of the day he went back to his room and slept for three hours. He rose at eight, boiled himself an egg, and began grading the fifty attempts at the letter of complaint.

At first he found himself unable to say anything about them: most had hardly begun, their efforts consisting of the salutation plus two or three sentences. There was one exception. It ran, *Dear Sir, I am amused by your attempt to perpetrate an obvious fraud on your unsuspecting customers. I am referring to the labelling of your eggs. Yesterday I bought a carton of "extra large" eggs of a size that would not have troubled a guinea-fowl. I wish to be fair, and besides I am interested. If you will produce a carton of "extra small" eggs, which by your standards will be marvels of miniaturization, I will not prosecute. You won't because you can't because you are scoundrels. Yours truly, R. Brown.*

William recognized immediately that R. Brown could become a problem. After consideration, he wrote, "Would not produce the desired effect," because the text said that the purpose of a business letter is to get the reader to do what you want. He read the letter through again and put a line through "unsuspecting" with the comment, "Avoid clichés." This got him started. On the others he wrote, "good beginning," "needs polish," "avoid jargon," and then, on every third letter, in the margin he wrote "awkward." He offered no grades so early in the semester.

On Tuesday he met two new classes, and on Wednesday his Monday classes returned. His Mondays, Wednesdays, and Fridays were the same, as were his Tuesday and Thursday mornings. He had Tuesday and Thursday afternoons off.

For his first class on Wednesday he delivered a little lecture on the salutation. He asked them all to think of a variant on "Dear Sir," and write it down. They talked about their suggestions at length and came to the conclusion that "Dear Sir" was best. They spent the last five minutes deciding where on the page it should be written. The Public Speaking class debated whether women were equal to men, and the Grammar class identified verbs. At lunch in the staff cafeteria on Wednesday, William, somewhat exhilarated, said to Spindle, "I find the Socratic mode very effective."

"What do you mean by that?" Spindle unpeeled the plastic from a tuna sandwich.

"You ask questions, and when you run out, you make each of *them* think of a question."

"A theory already! And it's only Wednesday. You'll be all right."

"How about you?"

"Me?"

"Yes. Are the classes going well?"

"As far as I know. You must understand, I'm involved with my subject, not with the students. Let me tell you a story. When I was in high school, the teachers were not allowed to smoke in the classroom, and one of the science masters, who was an addict, used to ignite the Bunsen burners by lighting a cigarette first and then using it as a spark. He usually got in four or five drags along the way, and we all knew what he was doing. I'm like that. Sometimes an interesting word crops up and I indulge myself for a couple of minutes. The difference between 'will' and 'shall' for example. I have a little joke about the Irishman who didn't know the difference and drowned as a result. Provided I don't go on too long they let me get away with it. About once a class I get in a few drags of this kind, and it's enough. But if I got involved with my classes I would probably go mad."

"Good old Geoff," said Bodger, who had joined them. "Very detached, he is. But I bet he's got some widow stashed away in Peterborough, eh, Geoff?"

"Jack doesn't believe that people are basically different," Spindle said. "He thinks that deep down they are all like him, interested only in money and frotting their bacon."

"That's right," Bodger said, puffing cheerfully on his pipe. "You can never get enough of both of them two. I knew a fellow once, in his sixties, he was . . ."

Maisie Clipsham appeared, and the talk turned to other things.

Thursday followed Wednesday, and on Friday William was astonished at how the week had disappeared. He said as much to Spindle when the department gathered for beer to celebrate the end of the week.

"Wait until February," Spindle said.

On Sunday the president held a reception for the faculty in the basement cafeteria of the Old Folks' Home. When William arrived he was met by a stout lady in a turban standing beside a coffee urn, Jocasta Cunningham, the president's wife.

"Where is your wife?" she asked him.

"I'm not married," William said.

She handed him a cup of coffee and took him by his free elbow, twisting him sharply away from her and spinning him into the room. He found himself face to face with the pretty winner of the shouting contest.

"Hello, Mr. Shy," she said.

"Your voice is quite low, really," William said, adding, "An excellent thing in a woman."

"I needed the job," she said. "I see by your presence it didn't make any difference, but you can never tell."

They were separated by a thin girl with shiny black hair. "I'm Jane Goray," she said. "I'm an old hand, here to make you feel at home. What can I tell you about dear old Van Horne?"

"Where is the Secretarial Science department?"

Jane Goray looked around the room. "George!" she called to a man standing by the coffee urn. "Come and join us." She turned back to them. "George is on duty today, too."

When he arrived, she said, "The lady wants to know where the Secretarial Science department is. Why don't you give her a tour?"

The sound of a piano broke in on their conversation. Dr. Cunningham was beginning a sing-song. The group of about a dozen that had so far arrived gathered self-consciously around the piano, while Mrs. Cunningham guarded the door.

"*Sleepy time gal*," the president sang.

"*Time gal*," the faculty muttered.

"*You're turning night into day* — sing up now."

The girl's hand touched William's and stayed. "How long did you plan to stay?" she asked him under cover of the song, and flashing a brilliant smile the length of the room as the president looked up from the keyboard.

"Two songs," William answered immediately. *"You'll dance the evening away.* What's the matter?"

"Mrs. Cunningham's got her eye on us. I live nearby. You go first and wait for me outside the Bible College. *You'll be a play-at-home, stay-at-home eight-o'clock sleepy time gal."*

The president banged a chord and started again. "Down by the Old Mill Stream," he called. *"Down by the old mill streeeeam."*

William waited until Mrs. Cunningham was busy with a new arrival and slid through the other door.

Her home turned out to be a coach house in the grounds of an old mansion, converted into a cosy apartment. The roof of the coach house had been made into a sun-deck, and here they sat, half-an-hour later, drinking gin-and-tonic.

"What's it like in Communication Arts?" she asked him.

William told her about his timetable and his colleagues, and politely asked the same question.

"About the same," she said. "I teach Clothing Design. That is, my timetable has fifteen hours of Sewing I on it. And three of Fabrics."

"What clothes are made of?"

"More or less." She leaned back and and closed her eyes, pulling her skirt up to her hips to allow her legs to catch the sun.

They had another drink.

"You have a very nice place here," he said.

"Want to see the rest of it?"

She showed him the living room, the kitchen, and the sun-warmed bedroom, which smelled of fresh linen. Later, after she had made them a rough *salade niçoise,* and they had drunk their coffee on the roof, she disappeared into the flat. When he found her, she was already in bed. Afterwards she said, "You will come back, won't you?"

"Of course. When?"

"End of next week. Phone first." She rolled over and composed herself for sleep.

He kissed her on the ear, and left.

iv. R. Brown

H E WAS MARKING exercises on the opening paragraph of the business letter, which, the text said, should be short and arresting. *Dear Sir*, the first one began, *You have won a million dollars.* The next paragraph began, *Wouldn't it be nice if this was true?*

William wrote, "The right idea but beware of reader backlash."

The next exercise began, *Dear Sir, Are you aware that a defalcation has been perpetrated in your accounts?* It continued, *Is this the language your present accountants use to announce or rather conceal the fact that you have a crook in your office? If so, you may wish to consider a change. Try us.* It was R. Brown again. William wrote, "Once again, you have sacrificed effectiveness for the sake of showing off. This letter would offend, I believe." Then he underlined "perpetrate" and wrote, "Do not overuse," adding "awk."

William had identified R. Brown now as an undersized boy with a wizened face and lank hair. He spoke as he wrote and was much admired by the other students. William was finding his very presence in the room like a silent mocking commentary on the quality and level of his teaching, though Brown had made no overt gesture of criticism. It was evident, though, that he would have to be confronted eventually. William talked to Spindle, who said, "If I were you, I would ignore his intelligence and ability, or you will soon find yourself consulting him. Continue to penalize him heavily for his failure to strike the right note in business correspondence. Make him realize that the classical skills will do him no good here."

William took the advice. Brown received his graded assignments with evident interest, read William's comments with a look of pleasure, and, with a nod of acknowledgement to William, dropped the exercises into the wastebasket on his way out.

In general, his teaching was going about as well as he could have hoped. The third week of term had begun and William had found an appropriate stance for all his classes. In the Public Speaking hours he simply announced the topics in advance, and sat through the little debates that followed. The Grammar classes munched steadily through the exercises. The Business Correspondence classes discussed a "problem" a day. Clem Stokes required that all new teachers be inspected very early by their colleagues, and he earned glowing reports from everybody when they observed that he used exactly the methods favoured by themselves: he drilled the Grammar class for Maisie Clipsham; he organized a panel discussion on the dangers of hitchhiking for Mordecai Redburn; and he discussed how to close a business letter with a "hook" when Jack Bodger came by. Geoffrey Spindle simply waved at him through the classroom door on the grounds that the early inspections were really just a kind of surveillance to make sure that William was present and sober.

By the end of the first month the work held no terrors at all. It was busy, even exhausting, so that if he was going out at night, he always took a nap for about an hour when he got home, but the time passed quickly enough in the classroom. R. Brown said to him one day, while they were waiting in the corridor for the previous class to vacate the room, "I must congratulate you, sir, on still being with us . . ." The rest of his remark was cut off by a fight in the doorway as the bell signalled the end of classes. Brown himself had not turned out to be such a problem after all. He was essentially benign, asking only to be allowed a small platform from time to time. Both his writing and his speaking style were utterly outside the range of everyone else in the room, but he had the quality of being able to excel without generating envy. The rest of the students were rather proud of him. William dealt with him as if he were seriously incapacitated through no fault of his own, ignoring Brown's taste and flair for felicitous sentences, and concentrating on the lack of effectiveness, in a business sense, of Brown's writing, all according to the best practice. Thus, when Brown managed a letter of abuse worthy of the young Swift, William failed him for alienating his correspondent, very occasionally adding, "Well written, though!" Brown accepted this, not at all interested in the grade apparently, but happy to be allowed to play. The other students followed Brown's lead in all things intellectual, and thus William became aware that, far from being faced with a problem, he had Brown to thank for the respect of the class. He took the opportunity one day to ask Brown why he was at Van Horne instead of a more classical academy.

Brown said, "I thought it behooved me to fit myself for the age of the technologist which is upon us. The age of the untrained educated man is over. You are a dodo, sir. I am the new man."

Spindle said, "He's probably right, though I resent his giving *you* the title of dodo."

v. Solidarity Forever

THE DAY AFTER Thanksgiving, the president of the Faculty
Association called a meeting. Spindle said, "Let's go. I
understand that great changes are afoot. You'll be able to
watch the politicians in action."

William was happy to belong to a union. Once he had been
asked if he was a true-blue Tory and had replied that he felt
more like a yellow socialist. He was pleased with the laugh it
raised and continued to use the term.

Like all meetings, it took place in the basement cafeteria of
the Old Folks' Home. It began with reports from committees:
flowers had gone to the funeral of a former colleague; ten
dollars had been sent to feed an orphan in Africa; a battle was
being waged to prevent the students using the staff lavatories.
Then the president of the association rose to speak. He was
a man, named Klopstock, who taught welding; a large man
with wavy red hair and a huge bunch of the tools of his trade
hanging from a steel ring at his waist. "I'm here to bring you
a proposal from the president," he said. He made it clear that
he had something momentous to say. In a brief speech, he
outlined for them a conversation he had had with Dr.
Cunningham in which the president had sought the coopera-
tion of the faculty in securing independent status for the
college.

"You mean we'd be like a regular college?" a voice asked.

"That's the size of it."

"Who would pay us?"

Klopstock explained some more. "The money would still come from the same place, but the president thinks it's time for us to be academically autonomous. Do what we like. But he needs our support to go to the government. Get a new charter."

"Would we be called 'professors'?" a little old lady who was knitting in the corner asked.

"If that's what turns us on, yes."

"Same holidays?"

"Same holidays."

The group was silent. All the important questions had been asked. Klopstock held up his hand, then began reading from a bit of paper. "I averred to Dr. Cunningham that we might be interested under the following terms: that the Faculty Association negotiate a contract with the management, such that membership in it be compulsory; that we get an immediate compensatory readjustment of twenty per cent to cover unforeseen disadvantages; that everyone get tenure; that salaries be negotiated every six months by the association; that no one be discriminated against on the grounds of paper qualifications; that cost-of-living raises be automatic; that class sizes be strictly limited to present medians; and that the months of June, July, August be designated 'study breaks.'"

"And what did Gravely say to that?" a woman with a sarcastic air asked.

Klopstock waited until the room was on edge. "He bought it," he said.

"Christ," the sarcastic woman said. "You should have asked him for luncheon vouchers, too."

Klopstock said, "He's very keen that we all march into the future together."

Talk began and turned into a hubbub. One or two instructors tried to ask other questions, but Klopstock adjourned the meeting to give the members time to "discuss it among yourselves." He would call for a vote at the next meeting after he had been able to offer further clarification on some of the questions.

On the way out William said to Geoffrey Spindle, "It seems rather a lot, doesn't it?"

Spindle said, "Worth it to the president, though, if he gets what he wants."

"What is that?"

Spindle waited until they were outside the building and in no danger of being overheard. "He wants his own university," he said. "To start with, a college that gives degrees."

"Here?" William looked back over his shoulder at the Old Folks' Home.

"It's not a new idea to me. Klopstock was telling us at lunch about his meeting with Cunningham. He said the president wants his own college so badly it's giving him a hard-on. That was Klopstock's expression. But he can't have it without our consent, because the faculty would refuse to go along unless we were guaranteed the same protection we have now. Thus we have him by the balls. This is Klopstock's language, you understand. Klopstock used to negotiate with General Motors. Apparently when you have someone like Cunningham by the balls you twist them, because he is unlikely to let you get that close again. I think I've got the figure right. Would you like to have a drink at my place?"

This last question came so suddenly that William became wary. Spindle was a very private man, and no one, so far as

William knew, had ever been invited home, although he lived only about four blocks from the institute. William feared some disclosure, at least, but it was impossible to refuse.

"Welcome to my lair," Spindle said when they reached the apartment.

But it was no more than the typical living quarters of any erudite bachelor. Books covered one wall; records and a record-player took up one corner; and the rest was furnished with armchairs and various kinds of lights. William relaxed slightly.

"Come in here for a moment and I'll show you my secret," Spindle called from an inner room. As William walked into the room, Spindle pointed to the bed. "There you are," he said. "Now you know it all." William felt a surge of alarm; Spindle's voice was proud and unnatural, but then William saw that he was pointing not to the bed as such, but to the coverlet, a superb quilt of tiny squares of different-coloured cloths, obviously, even to William, a work of great skill and patience if not high art. Then he saw it all.

"You made it, Geoffrey?"

"I made it. I have been making them for years. I sewed my first ones in hospital years ago, and I became addicted. Now I make a square a day, four or five quilts a year."

"What do you do with them?"

"I sell them to a shop downtown, pretending they are made by my old mother. My old mother, in fact, plays canasta all day. Would you like one? I've never given one to anyone before for fear of being exposed."

"Oh, I don't think so. I move about too much."

"Then let's not mention the subject again. But now you know why I have so few visitors. I must quilt. If I don't do my square a day I get miserable. But if word got around my

Industrial Arts classes, I might have some trouble keeping order. I am completely in your power now." He looked hard at William.

"Don't worry, Geoff. Not a word." William searched for a change of topic. "How long have you known that Dr. Cunningham had the idea of a university in mind?"

"From the beginning. He and I arrived at Van Horne more or less at the same time."

"Did he hire you?"

"Not exactly. But shortly after he arrived I became aware that he saw the role of the institute in rather more expanded terms than others did. That was about when he changed his title from principal to president. Our job, as the deputy minister explained it to me, was to make further — not higher — education available to more voters' children, to — er — take the students the universities didn't want, as one of the academicians across the road put it to me. Cunningham sees a different future. He says we are taking the students who don't want them." Spindle clapped his hands to clear the air. "Now. You're assured that I don't have designs on you, so let's have another beer, eh? And perhaps you will come again," he concluded with a mixture of arrogance and shyness.

After that, William spent a couple of evenings a week with his new friend, drinking a bottle of beer while Spindle sewed his quota for the night. It was like visiting a learned and favourite aunt.

vi. The Strange Case
of Mordecai Redburn

H IS OTHER COLLEAGUES were just as forthcoming. Bodger dreamed of making a lot of money; his wife kept a shop which sold knick-knacks to the tourist trade, and Bodger spent most of his time there, when he was free of teaching. He constantly proposed schemes to William "as a likely kind of guy"; schemes for making their fortunes. William had always suffered from a chameleon-like appearance of receptivity to ideas, and even ways of life, that were unthinkable to him. Religious maniacs sensed a convert; lechers invited him to hunt in pairs; travelling ladies found him safe, while across the carriage, travelling salesmen winked at his cleverly concealed satyriasis. All the world claimed him as kin. Even Maisie Clipsham sent out messages that she might welcome the advances of someone as well washed as he.

Mordecai Redburn was the most forthcoming of all. One night over supper in the Chicken Chalet, after an extra bottle of beer, the two bachelors talked of love.

"A ladies' man, are you?" Mordecai asked with elaborate casualness.

As always, Wiliam found the sympathetic answer, guessing that Redburn was not very successful in love. "Not really," he said. "I have to work hard for what I get."

"Like *me*." Mordecai beamed. "No, let me be absolutely honest. Would you believe this?" His eyes twinkled under his bright grey thatch. "I'm a virgin. Forty-two and never, as Jack Bodger would say, dipped my wick. Like Yeats. But I've never wanted to!" He grew excited. "Let's have another beer. My treat." When the beer arrived and was half drunk, he brushed away William's attempts to change the subject. "Until recently, I'd never understood what all the fuss was about. I've never had any interest in life down there. At school, when the other boys made jokes, and more — I went to a private school where they talked endlessly about it, and practised what they preached, as far as I knew — I nodded and winked to be part of the crowd, but I had no real idea what they were talking about. Not that I am deficient. I've had a lot of tests — am I going it a bit strong? You don't mind, do you? I just never had any desire, or any desire to create desire, if you know what I mean. I think it's linked with another side of me, equally inhuman, if I can use the word in its literal, non-pejorative sense. I have no friends, nor have I ever had any, or needed any. I receive invitations to go to dinners and parties — my family is well connected — but I never feel what is called lonely, which I believe means pain at being alone. Just the opposite, in fact. My parents used to be on at me constantly to join the human race, as they called it. They wanted me to show any kind of mating instinct, but I never did. I think I must be a kind of tryffid, or a psychological sport. That's why I wondered if you were a bit of a tryffid yourself. In the book, all the tryffids know each other."

"No," William said firmly. "Friendship and sex are both important to me."

"Really. And yet I feel closer to you than I have with anyone."

"But surely that contradicts what you've been saying?"

"Ah. Now to the present. All I've been telling you is history, not to be repeated to a living soul." He leaned excitedly over the table. "Recently I have begun to learn that I'm leaving the tryffid state behind. There are stirrings in the underbrush, signs of spring. I think now I've been a kind of Sleeping Beauty, and I'm waking up. A few months ago my mother, who feels responsible for me still, persuaded me to see a psychiatrist, although I told her there was nothing whatever the matter with me. I was happier than she has ever been. Nevertheless, this man thought he could treat me, so I went along with it. I thought it might add a dimension to my reading of *Madame Bovary*. Essentially, he's put me on a course of behaviour re-inforcement. He has introduced me artificially to the miseries of aloneness and the pleasures of gregariousness, reinforcing them with chemicals, so that I have had an experience of pain grafted on, so to speak. For the first time in my life, I find that talking to you like this is more pleasurable than solving chess problems. That's why I sought you out for dinner. I haven't even had a pill, and it's being quite nice. Do you mind? I thought perhaps we might have the odd bite together, and then I could move on to other people." Redburn suggested this with the air of an eleven-year-old proposing that the two of them become buddies.

"Of course, Mordecai. But what about . . . the other thing?"

"Can I trust you entirely?"

"Certainly."

"He is teaching me to masturbate and like it; something you've been doing since you were a child, I expect."

"From time to time," William said, wondering if there was any chance they could be overheard. "Not incessantly. Then not at all."

"Ah, yes, intercourse. My shrink said, first I've got to learn to like myself, and then I could move on to the next stage."

"How long will it take?" Forty-two seemed very late to start life.

"He doesn't know. He's never had a patient like me. He thinks I will make his name."

"Do you like it?"

"What?"

"Doing it. By yourself?" Soon, William thought, someone will fling a curtain aside and shout, "Okay, you two. Out!"

Mordecai said, "I'm starting to. Better yet, I have an urge to, from time to time."

"That's great. Isn't it?"

"Yes. The only trouble is it's not properly responsive yet. Pornography doesn't work, but I can get an erection talking on the phone to my father. All sorts of odd times. My shrink says it's because I'm listening too hard. He's sure I will soon be conditioned into convenient urges, when I'm alone. Like you."

They finished their dinner and Redburn insisted on paying the bill. "I knew you'd understand," he said, as they walked away from the restaurant. "That's what friends are for. And you're my first."

"There'll be lots more, I'm sure."

Meanwhile William and Jane continued an arrangement that was comfortable and satisfying without any suggestion that it was more than that for either of them. Nothing like it had ever happened to him before. For two years he had lived very intensely among a small group of graduate English students. He had had two girlfriends in Canada. The most recent had been a girl named Gloria who had been a student in one of his seminars at Simcoe, and then enrolled as a graduate student at

McGill because her family had moved to Montreal. They had chatted at length about what the separation meant, and agreed that they were uncertain of their feelings for each other, and therefore a period of separation would help them to bring their relationship into focus. They corresponded regularly, and became good friends by mail, but were waiting still for further guidance.

The simplicity of his affair with Jane was hard to get used to after the elaborately verbalized relationships he had had with Gloria and her predecessor. It took him several weeks to realize and admit to himself that she was his mistress, that nothing else was required of him except to bring the wine and make love. In fact, she refused to allow him any further access to her life; they never appeared together outside the apartment. He wondered often if there were not some Gothic presence in the background, even a promise made on a death-bed, that could account for her stance, but in time he came to realize that she was simply taking care of herself in the way she wanted. If she was his mistress, then he, in a sense, was hers. He felt he ought to be demeaned, culturally, if not personally, but he experienced none of the usual symptoms indicating that his manhood was threatened, so for the moment he set such thoughts aside and accepted her as the actualization of a youthful fantasy. They treated each other with respect, and the demands they made were only those of courtesy.

vii. The End of Dunvegan

"I THINK OUR chairman is becoming restless," Spindle said one day as he trimmed a square of scarlet rayon. "If you find yourself with anything I can use, let me have it, will you? I get what I can at the Salvation Army, but a really good bit, one of your old silk dressing gowns, say, would be very welcome."

"My only dressing gown is made of a kind of blanket material, but you can have it soon. What's this about Scyld Dunvegan? What do you mean — 'restless'?"

"He's sniffing the west wind, hearing the cry of the wild goose. He's on the move."

"Where to?"

"I don't know, but he's been lunching out a lot lately, and there have been several calls from some heavy-sounding gents. Either he's involved in a conspiracy, or he's looking for another job."

"Where would he go from here? Another college?"

"I doubt that. He's a shrewd cookie, our Scyld, and he can read omens. He knows the next cycle is beginning. People like you are the end of people like him."

"Me? What have I done? I'm just grateful for the job. He hired me."

"You are the first person to come to us with more or less the right qualifications. For me, this place was a refuge from the storm. I am unqualified by being overqualified. Jack Bodger used to be about right, but he won't be good for much longer unless he can get into administration. Even Mordecai had better get some kind of M.A., perhaps in Education, if he plans to stay. You, on the other hand, are just sufficiently over qualified to be one of the group that will move the institute into its next phase. One day you will be replaced by a Ph.D. in Communications Theory, but you should be good for some time yet."

"Are we talking about Van Horne?"

"We are. We are talking about the inevitable process that will result in this place becoming an institute of higher learning. One of the signs is that motion passed in the Commercial Science council last week, deploring the president's suggestion that there should be a modicum of liberal arts in their curriculum. This is a practical institution, they insist. If a businessman wants Shakespeare he can drive to Stratford, they say. No need to waste the taxpayers' money, they cry. The fact is, some of those people can smell the future and they are terrified."

"Is Dunvegan frightened, too?"

"Not like that. But he's got good instincts. He can feel that the game is up, and he has no intention of becoming one of those pathetic relics left over from a previous era that one finds in evolutionary situations. He's working on his next move."

"What will he do? What's he qualified for? Private school?"

"His pals will find something for him. Scyld belongs to an informal fraternity that I'll call Oxbridge-on-the-St. Lawrence. It consists of all those members of the establishment who have spent a term at Oxford or Cambridge. The aristocrats of the society are the Rhodes scholars, but it is a large body, and includes some people who only managed to wangle a card at the Bodleian in order to follow a program of private study and learn to punt on the Cherwell. Like Gatsby, these people return to Canada and dream afterwards about their Oggsford days, and even try to keep them alive among themselves. They would like to live in a college with a porter's gate and a master and college servants, and they socialize together. I believe there is even a club. But most of all they form a freemasonry; they *know* each other. And they do things together, especially government things, because there is no job so suitable for a life of dreaming about Oxford as that of an assistant deputy minister. The members of this fraternity look after their own. They have jobs to dispose of, from university registrars all the way down to secretaries of arts councils. Wherever it's felt that a particular job would benefit from a touch of Oxbridge, there you'll find one of the boys."

"But what are Dunvegan's qualifications?"

"He was once a physical education major, and a first-rate athlete. He rowed for a college at Oxford, where he had managed to get enrolled in a theology diploma. Now, of course, his chief qualification is membership of the Oxbridge club."

William pondered the possible effect of this on his own life. "Who will replace him, Geoffrey?"

Spindle tacked the edge of the material and bit the thread off neatly. "That's the question, isn't it? Let's look at the possibilities. Jack Bodger? No. I don't think I'm a snob, except intellectually, but we need a bit more style than Bodger. Mordecai? I don't know what's up with Mordecai, these days. He is like a man who is secretly hiding an escaped convict in the cellar. Thoroughly self-absorbed, but I don't know what about, and obviously not in the frame of mind to lead us anywhere. Maisie? Not unthinkable, but not yet. Anyway, Clem Stokes wouldn't have her. He was in the navy. He thinks women are unlucky. Who else? Not me, certainly. I have enough to entertain me, and life never cast me in a role like that. I prefer to sit on the bank and watch. Which leaves you, or a stranger."

"Don't be silly. I've only been here two months."

"Two months is a long time around here."

"You really think so?"

"That two months is a long time? Oh, you mean you? I think that the logic of it will fill Stokes's head as it has filled mine. You are young without looking like a baby; you have an M.A. of sorts; you are personable, and without obvious vices. You have class, Bodger says, meaning, I think, tone. It's the Cambridge accent, probably. Still desirable in sub-academic circles like these for the quality that Bodger has identified, although I suspect you haven't got long. I hear ancestral voices prophesying war coming out of the graduate school. One day, when jobs are harder to get, you'll find your accent works against you. An organization of out-of-work graduate students will write a manifesto saying our youth is being corrupted by foreign professors. It's inevitable. In the meantime you are in the driver's seat. It would be better if you were married, but we can't have everything. All you lack is ambition."

So William became ambitious.

The Director of Humane Studies said to the president, "There's only one of them you could dress up and pass off as a chairman: the new guy, Moodie."

"I sometimes wonder, Clem, if you make enough allowance for the fact that academics are often eccentric."

"There's nothing academic or eccentric about this bunch, except for Spindle. The rest of them are just out of it."

"Why not Spindle, then? We came to Van Horne together, you know."

"He's got enough sense to know his limits. He recommends Moodie."

"You've consulted him, have you? Good. All right, tell this Moodie you want to see him about something, and I'll come by the office and take a peek at him."

At the end of November the president announced that, as of January, Mr. Scyld Dunvegan would be leaving to take up new duties as the principal of an Approved Boys' School. "We must regret his abrupt departure and the loss to the institute, but the request for his services from the ministry was very urgent," Cunningham said, "and we must not stand in his way. To replace him we are taking the unusual step of appointing someone fairly new to the institute. But it is at the urging of his colleagues, and with the support of his former chairman, that the Director of Humane Studies has recommended it to me, so I am happy to announce that the new chairman will be Mr. William Moodie, with effect from January the first."

Later that night, all passion temporarily spent, Jane said, "Does this mean you'll be too grand for me now?"

"Not at all. It'll mean I shall have more leisure for you. Dunvegan didn't spend much time in the classroom."

"That's all right then. I could be helpful. It's lonely at the top. You'll need someone to talk to. Now, tell me what happened at the president's meeting."

And so there began a practice, an expectation, of a leisurely post-coital chat about his week's activities. He talked and she listened, interested in even the smallest details of his new world. Very occasionally he sought her advice, mainly on the manners and behaviour appropriate for his position. (Van Horne was a long way from Cambridge, in every sense.) For example, did she agree with another chairman that it was risky for William to have a glass of ale with his lunch, because if Clem Stokes smelled it on his breath, he would assume that William had spent most of the day in a beer parlour? On the whole, she did. Clem Stokes, she reminded him, was from Alberta, where it would have been a reasonable assumption. Usually, she said nothing, and he worried from time to time that he was boring her, but she assured him that she would tell him as soon as that was the case.

Jack Bodger said, when he heard of William's appointment, "A good number you've got yourself. Is there an expense allowance?"

Maisie Clipsham said, "Perhaps now we can get the floor swept occasionally."

Mordecai said, "We will still be able to have supper together sometimes, won't we?"

Geoffrey Spindle said, "If you buy a new wardrobe, I'd like the shirt you are wearing to finish off a corner."

R. Brown said, "If you could be persuaded not to hand over our class to someone else, we would swear undying gratitude."

viii. A New Calendar

CHRISTMAS WAS COMING and bringing with it the first taste of loneliness and homesickness William had experienced since he arrived in Canada. The two previous Christmases had passed pleasantly enough in the company of Gloria and his student pals, enough of whom were married to provide a more or less continuous house-party from Christmas Eve to New Year's Day. Cut off from that, and from Gloria, who was spending the holiday skiing in Banff, he began to wonder what to do, and even contemplated flying home to spend the time with his widowed father. He had never been very close to his father, but coming to Canada had created a desire, like that experienced by soldiers in wartime, to reforge the conventional bond, and he had begun to write conscientiously, once a month, detailing his pleasure in his new country and, lately, his success in his first career. They were long letters, self-consciously diarizing his day-to-day activities. He tried to "catch" the new characters he was encountering, creating little portraits to amuse his father. In this way he described his encounters with an Irish panhandler, an Ojibway family selling blueberries at a gas station on the highway, an old Italian knife-grinder who walked the streets ringing a bell like a pieman, and a mad Estonian woman who paraded in national costume on the downtown streets, shouting at passers-by in her native tongue.

He enjoyed writing these sketches, and after he had got the habit, he started to keep a copy of the letters for the future. He did not flatter himself that he was any more than an amateur writer, but he worked hard at the letters, and thought that some day they might, just possibly, be worth collecting into a little book. Something for his children, at least.

Usually his father replied in three or four short sentences within a month. "Hope all goes well. There's no money in teaching. Have you thought of going into insurance? Keep well wrapped up." Another said, "Keep it up. Any thought of getting spliced? Looking forward to my grandchildren, ha-ha. All well here. Got the telly now."

This time the response came by return of mail. His father was planning to spend the season in Sicily with his new girlfriend. Perhaps William could come at Easter?

And then, on the Saturday before Christmas, he found what he wanted in the travel section of the morning paper, a country inn which offered three days of merry-making for an all-in price, singles welcome. Here he spent the holiday, eating and drinking. He was not the only "single," but he was younger by twenty years than any of the others, and he was content to spend the days reading in front of the log fire.

"Assume a virtue if you have it not, and pretty soon you find you have it. That's what we're doing. Oh, I know we are pretty thin on the ground so far. Not all the faculty will be able to meet the challenge of the coming decade, but we're building a team, Moodie, and you are on the team. We shall sink one basket at a time. Don't forget, Harvard started as a Bible college."

They were sitting in the president's office, having the first of many, many meetings, as the president took William into his confidence. He spoke now through a steady rain of nods,

punctuated by an occasional sideways swoop of the head.
When he paused, the nodding continued, like an engine tick-
ing over. "Now, what are you going to do for us, eh? First of
all, some new courses, more appropriate to our development.
Next year we're going to have a proper calendar and we don't
want to be continually changing it, so let's anticipate what the
next few years will bring. These courses here — are they
what we want to look like? English: Writing I, Writing II, and
Writing III. And then Oral I, Oral II, and Oral III. Then the
same thing for Business Correspondence. Not very scintillat-
ing, is it?"

"We have those two as well." William pointed down the
list. "'Stories for Today' and 'Stories for the Ages.' That's
short stories and fairy stories."

"They sound a bit simple-minded, even for us. I was looking at the calendars of some American colleges the other day.
Let's have something with 'Types' in it. 'Types of Prose
Fiction: The Short Story' — that kind of thing. Then you
might have 'Types of Prose Fiction II: The Novel,' and so on.
Get the description ready for the calendar, and then one day
we can offer them. Most colleges never plan ahead far enough;
their calendars are always out of date."

William scribbled busily. "What about fairy stories? It's all
Miss Clipsham teaches, apart from grammar. I think the
course is very popular."

"Call it 'Gods and Gargoyles: A Survey of the Fabulous in
Fiction.' Then you can put in anything. Now I seem to be
doing all the work. What suggestions do you have?"

"'Man in Action: A History of Drama,'" William suggested.

"Good. Keep going."

"'Songs and Sonnets'?"

"Bit dull. More."

"'Archetypes: Images of Form'?"

"That's better. Now one with 'thought' in it. They always have a few of them."

"'The Passionate Years: A Survey of Mid-Twentieth-Century Thought.'"

"That's *very* good. Is it original?"

"I just made it up."

"Well done. Now, rework the titles of the courses you people are presently teaching and we shall have done a good morning's work. What about Canadian Literature? I notice that none of our post-secondary rivals around here have much of that in their calendars. Perhaps we could be the first."

"I'll find out about it, sir."

"I've enjoyed this, Moodie. The other divisions don't offer the same creative scope."

"We seem to be moving a bit faster than I anticipated," Geoffrey Spindle said. "You're right, this dressing gown's a bit hairy for my purposes. No, no. Don't worry about it. I'll find a use for it." He hung the dressing gown up in his closet. "I don't know that Bodger or our students are quite ready for — what was it? — 'Images of Form'? But no doubt the students will be when Bodger is. I take it I'm now to start failing students who can't read or write?"

"Don't be too hasty. I think the president wants us to create an upward pressure rather than make any abrupt changes. The president wanted to know about Canadian Literature. Could we put together a course? I know Stephen Leacock, of course. What else is there?"

"There's two kinds, I think. There's a bit of poetry, actually quite a bit, starting around the turn of the century, and there are the novels they take in school. I don't think there are any plays, but I may be wrong. At any rate, there isn't an awful lot, and I think you'll find that the high schools have got most of it. Apart from that, there's a kind of ur-literature — diaries, letters, essays in newspapers — you know the sort of thing? Nothing remotely teachable to our students. Sort of thing that's best left to the graduate schools — 'Prairie Literature: The Origins' — courses like that. I think we'll have to wait until some more is written."

Maisie said, "I suppose I am going to have to find out all about 'myth'?"

"It's just the title that's changed, not what you teach."

Bodger said, after asking a number of questions, "Don't get me wrong. I *like* literature."

In time, the new calendar appeared, and there for two full pages, the department's courses were listed and described, each with a new number and a little remark in parentheses, like "(Some previous acquaintance with psychology an asset)."

"Exciting, isn't it," Mordecai said. "We could leave this about for people to see."

ix. The Man Who Knew Dylan

ENROLMENT WAS ON the increase, and William was given permission to hire two more teachers. Five applicants responded to an advertisement in the newspaper. The first was a Welshman, a man of about sixty, dirty, strong-smelling, who claimed to have known Dylan. "I knew Dylan well," he said when William asked him to talk about himself. "We didn't know at the time that he was going to be the great man. They picked me for that. How long have you had this job, then? All right, is it?" He looked around the plywood cubicle appraisingly.

William ignored the questions. "What is your speciality, Mr. Jennings?"

Jennings grinned. "Same as yours, man. Looking after number one. But we won't talk about it. If you mean, what can I teach, I can teach anything. What do you have? What's the job worth, anyway? I'd expect a bit of preferment with my background. I'm imported, like you. Goes down well over here. They put it on jars of marmalade." He winked. "You've done well for yourself. These colonials don't know they're born, do they?"

William said, "Here's a form. If you would fill it out and leave it, I'll get in touch with you."

Jenning's face went black. "Stick your form up your arse, man. I'm here to do you a favour. You don't tell a man who knew Dylan when you were in nappies to fill out a bloody form!" He stood up and addressed Mordecai Redburn and Jack Bodger through the open door. "This fella will do you in. I've seen his kind before."

"There's no point in filling out the form now," William said. "Would you please leave?"

"At your age I had more respect," Jennings said, and walked out kicking the wastebasket ahead of him.

When he was gone, Mordecai said, "While he was waiting to see you, he asked me to lend him twenty dollars until pay-day."

"Did you?"

"Yes."

The next applicant was a neatly dressed man in his forties with his hair cut very short and large military-looking black shoes. He lacked actual teaching experience, having recently switched from government work to English Studies. His name was Murray Penzler.

"What did you do with the government?" William asked him.

Penzler got up and closed the door. "I'm speaking confidentially?" he asked.

"If you want."

"I do want, sir. You see I was engaged in duties of an anti-subversive nature."

"What does that mean?"

"I worked for an agency of the Defence ministry. Security."

"A policeman?"

Penzler got up from his chair, and picked up the phone, listening closely. Then he put it down outside the cradle, waited, and banged the receiver on the table twice, listened again, then replaced it. "I was attached to the Mounties," he said, quietly. "You won't find any record of it in the files, though."

"What happened?"

"Burnout."

"So you took up literature?"

"Right. Remember, this is confidential. Let's just put down that I was in a monastery."

"That won't stop people from being curious. But why couldn't you have carried on doing other work? In the office, perhaps."

"No more questions, do you mind? I'm a teacher now." He smiled warmly at William.

William looked at Penzler's record. The references were all from very distinguished Canadian scholars. "You've done well since you left the government."

"Those guys know how to write a letter, don't they?"

"We need you next week. Is that possible?"

"I'm used to leaving in half-an-hour. One thing, I'd like you to take this number." He passed a slip of paper across the desk. "If you can't find me at any time, call that number and when they answer, just say 'Penzler's gone.' They'll know what to do."

"You mean you still work for them? That's surely going to interfere with your classes, isn't it?"

Penzler cut him off. "No, I'm not still active. But there are, or may be, guys still looking for me." He got up and took another slip of paper from his wallet. "If you want me in the ordinary way, I'll be staying at this number. It's a residential hotel run by a retired interrogator."

The other three candidates were all people like William, recently dropped out of the same graduate school. He recognized two of them, a specialist in Early English Drama and a man doing a thesis on Frederick Philip Grove, and rejected them immediately, hiring a third, unknown to him before, a student of Browning who called him "sir" repeatedly.

x. Mordecai, Mostly

A S A CHAIRMAN, William came into much closer contact
with the director, Clem Stokes. Weekly meetings were
held to discuss the policies of the division, attended by
William and the chairman of the Related Studies department,
Henry Doberman. Here the three administrators plotted strat-
egy for the division.

"We have two concerns," Stokes said by way of introducing
William to divisional policy. "Get teachers in the classroom
who won't rock the boat, and keep the big fella upstairs
happy." He pointed to the ceiling.

"God?" William asked, remembering Jane's remark that
Stokes came from the prairies.

"Him, too," Stokes said. "But I meant El Presidente. Give
him what he wants and we'll be all right."

Stokes went on to explain how the chairman was to keep
track of teachers who were sick, and the importance of surprise inspections. "You don't have to go into the room," he
said. "But let them see you are around. Walk past the door a
couple of times a day." He looked at his watch. "That's enough
for now. I have to take my car in."

Afterwards, Doberman said, "No, we don't talk a helluva
lot about education, I agree, but he doesn't try to run the division on sound business principles like Katesmark over in

Commercial Science. Katesmark calls his chairmen 'middle managers.' Last year they had to produce budgets according to a system of priorities. They had to grade each activity by how essential it was and buy as many activities as they had money for. Chairmen turned out to be most essential: after these came secretaries, then janitors, I think. Teachers came very low, but it didn't matter because all the teachers are permanent civil servants. In the end they drew up budgets just like us, but Katesmark said it was a good exercise. He said the system works well for the aircraft industry in Oklahoma."

Once a month Dr. Cunningham held a meeting of his administrators, about thirty in all, and gave them a little talk. At the first of these that William attended, the president spoke of the future. "When you people are out of work," he said, nodding gently around the room, and smiling at the effect of his words as soon as he spoke them, "I'll be happy. If you do your job of taking Van Horne into the future, none of you will be qualified when the future arrives. Of course I'm exaggerating. There's no real chance that you will make yourselves out-of-date . . ."

"None, buddy, none," said a voice in William's ear.

". . . but that should be your objective. We've got to reach beyond our grasp until Van Horne is equal to the best."

"Look at him," said the voice. "Leading us out of the wilderness, he is."

William turned and saw the chairman of the Building Trades department looking earnestly up at Cunningham, nodding along with him. Without changing his devout expression, or looking away from the president, he said to William. "He's what they call a visionary. Very destructive of the status quo, they are." He gave the president four or five nods, and added,

"He'll be talking about the good of the institute next — there he goes — I've got some news for him: what's good for me is good for Van Horne. Hear, hear." The last words, accompanied by vigorous hand-clapping, were spoken at the conclusion of the president's speech. With an elaborate Artful Dodger grimace to William, the chairman left.

"I think I told you I'm seeing a psychiatrist?" Mordecai asked rhetorically.

They were having their weekly supper together, their first, however, for three weeks, as William had been busy sorting out his new duties. Mordecai continued. "A rather odd thing happened to me. You remember he was teaching me to masturbate, or rather, to *want* to; I knew *how*, of course. Well, I got on all right with that, and I soon became normal. No more sudden urges when I was gardening — that sort of thing. Just when I'm reading, or when I wake up. My shrink says that's about right. Is it?" Mordecai appealed to him, *l'homme moyen sensuel*.

"I should say so."

"I mean, in your experience, that's how it takes people?"

"It sounds about right."

Mordecai nodded. "Now," he said, "a rather odd thing has started to happen. Just when I thought I understood it all, the physiology of it, I mean, I find I'm being distracted by other things. Or the absence of them."

"I'm not following you."

"There is something missing. And I think I know what. I have begun to find myself not terrifically happy by myself any more, except, of course, when I'm in heat — is that the right term? No? Well, contrary to what I told you about not understanding loneliness, I now understand it very well, one form anyway. It is the absence of the person you want to be with."

"Sounds as if you're in love. That's nice, Mordecai. Quick, too."

"I'm not sure if 'love' is the right word, though it might be. I just feel this overwhelming desire to be in a certain person's company, to talk to them, to share my life with them."

"That sounds fine. Anyone in particular?"

"No, that's the trouble. I think I'm in love with love itself. Think back. Did you ever go through anything like this?"

"Only as a teenager."

"That's what I am."

"Ah, well then. You are now going through the worst time of your life, psychologically speaking. It does end, though, in about two years, when you become an adult. In your case, that should happen in a few weeks, shouldn't it? Just hang on. Most people survive it."

"God, you are a comfort."

"I'm glad, but don't forget that I'm not a teenager. I can't talk all night." He looked at his watch. "I'm due elsewhere at this very moment."

"At least let me buy us another drink. Waiter, bring us two . . ." — Mordecai searched for an appropriate drink — "Tia Marias and some more coffee. I don't like spirits much, but this tastes quite nice."

Jane Goray was putting the final touches to a *frittata*, delicately browning the top. "I think this is done," she said. She put it on the table in its pan, and added bread and salad to the board. William opened a bottle of British Columbia white, poured some into two glasses, and they helped themselves to food.

"This is very good, as always," William said, his mouth full.

"But I wish you'd let me take you to a restaurant occasionally, now that I'm rich. I don't know what difference it could make."

"It would mean we were dating, and I told you that I won't go on dates with you. You aren't my type. Just bring the wine and I'll take care of everything else."

"But what if Mr. Right came along?"

"Then you'd find the door locked. In the meantime, doesn't this suit you?"

"I think it's wonderful. All of it."

"Well, then."

Afterwards they did the dishes and watched television for an hour before going to bed. And after that, she asked, "Now. Post coitus. Are you in love with me at all? Do you ever think of me between acts? Don't you want to know what time it is? Honestly now."

"That's all true. But I do like it here."

"Good. I like it here, too. But don't start getting sentimental about it. Now tell me what happened at the president's meeting. Then you'll have to go. I have an early class."

And so he told her about his growing awareness of the president's ambitions, of his desire to create an institution that all the present staff would be unqualified to teach in.

When he trailed off, she said, "Presumably, if he was saying this to you, then you would still be qualified."

"For a long time to come, that was my impression."

"That's all right, then." She pulled him towards her. "Now, once more, then I have to go to sleep. I have an eight o'clock. No, don't lie down. Like this."

xi. Penzler

A WEEK LATER William faced his first staff problem. Three students asked to see him when he was reading his mail. They had a complaint, they said, about an instructor. William seated them around the desk and closed the door.

"What's the trouble?" he asked, pleased that one of the problems he was paid to deal with had materialized at last.

"It's Mr. Penzler," the spokesman, a youth with a huge nose and no chin, said. The other two sat slightly behind him and watched him carefully, as if they expected him to make a run for it.

"What's the trouble between you and Mr. Penzler?"

The youth looked at the other two; they nodded at him to get on with it. "He doesn't come to classes." The other two nodded. "He only came . . . once." More nods. "The first day. We haven't seen him since."

"At all?" Classes were in their third week.

Now the youth with the nose made clear by his attitude that he had done his share. He looked at each of the others in turn, directing them, first with his left shoulder, then with his right, to speak.

Finally one of his escorts spoke. "We thought he was sick," he said in a loud metallic voice, so that William jumped.

"We've seen him in the cafeteria," the second escort said, bitterly.

"No, he's not sick as far as I know. Right. I'll find out. You go back to your classes and come back and see me on" — he looked at his calendar — "Friday. If nothing has changed, that is. There's probably a good explanation. I'm very glad you came and told me."

After the students had gone, he went to look for Penzler. He found him in the staff lounge.

"What did they look like?" Penzler asked. "Was their leader a guy with a big hooter? Drools a bit?"

"Yes."

"He's trouble. You've met the type. I knew on the first day he would try something like this. Let me explain. That class is working on a project. For the first two weeks I've assigned them a series of questions about the function of literature, questions they have to research. I act as a resource person. They know where to find me when they have a problem. In the meantime, I have more time to spend with my other groups who need a different approach. Don't let that trio fool you. I saw plenty of them in the army. The rest of the class are working, I'm pretty sure. That kid with the hooter, though, I may have to get rid of him."

"Request his transfer to another class, you mean?"

"For a start."

"When will you return to class? Formally, I mean."

"Tomorrow they all have to report back on what they've found out, and then I reassign them. I was just working on their next assignment." He held up a tiny notebook in which he had been making marks on a page.

"I see. That's all right, then. But you will respond to complaints, won't you?"

"I'll take care of them, don't worry."

On Friday the three students came back. They wanted a transfer to another group. Penzler, they said, had appeared the day before, dismissed the rest of the class, and spent the hour questioning the three of them to find out just what they were up to. They were very frightened and determined to get out of his way.

William looked over the timetable and transferred them to one of Spindle's classes. The next day he received a three-page letter from Penzler with a copy to his (Penzler's) lawyer asking him to sign an acknowledgement that William had arbitrarily and without consultation transferred students from Penzler to another instructor; that Penzler was not to be deemed, therefore, in any way deficient; and that he, William, was completely satisfied with Penzler's teaching.

William consulted Clem Stokes, who said, "Tell him to stick his letter up his arse. He's still on probation."

To Penzler, William said, "I don't think this is appropriate. Let's start again. You teach the students the courses as outlined and go to the classroom every day and I'll forget about these three."

Penzler smiled. "You're smart. Consolidate your position, Show these guys you've read the manuals, too." He pointed through the door to Mordecai and Jack Bodger. "I admire that."

The following week two other students came to him to complain about Penzler. Once more the complaint was that he had not appeared to teach his classes for some days. This time William realized he had not even seen Penzler in the office since the week before. He placated the students and sent them on their way, and did a quick tour of the likely places where Penzler might be found. He was nowhere in sight. William returned to his office, closed the door, and phoned the number Penzler had given him for emergencies. When the receiver was lifted at the other end, he said, "Penzler's gone."

"I had to do a test run," Penzler said. "Make sure my route was clear. Now I know I can trust you, I'll give you the real number tomorrow."

The next day Penzler was waiting for him when he arrived at the department. "I understand you had a couple of students in. What are their names? I'll handle them. You won't have any more trouble. By the way, you may be being watched. Don't worry about it. It's me they'll be looking for. I'll keep them off." Penzler shook hands and left.

After three more days with no further sign of Penzler, William went the rounds of his classes. One or two students turned up for each class, but evidently without much hope of seeing their instructor. It was as if his courses had died. William telephoned once more the number that Penzler had given him. There was no reply. He then phoned the hotel, where someone confirmed that Penzler lived there and promised to give him a message. That afternoon, lacking a reply, William went to the hotel and explained his problem to the manager. Together they went to Penzler's room, which the manager opened with his passkey. There was no sign of Penzler. The room had been used, but Penzler was gone.

William's phone rang as he returned to his office. "Don't worry," Penzler said. "I've shaken them, I'm pretty sure. I'll be in to work tomorrow or the day after."

"No you won't," William said. "I'm assigning your classes to someone else. Give me an address and I'll forward your cheque."

"You do this and you'll have a lot to answer for, Moodie."

"All right," William said.

"Ottawa, I mean."

"All right."

There was a long pause. Then, "Send the cheque here, to the hotel. I'll have it picked up tonight. In the meantime, Moodie, under no circumstances are you to discuss me with anyone. Understood?"

"I have to say why you're gone."

"Say something medical. And Moodie, watch yourself. Those guys — Bodger and Redburn — don't let them get behind you. They'd like to see you fall. It wouldn't be hard. I ran a check on you. Do they know what's in your file?"

William put down the phone and looked at Penzler's timetable. At the end of the day he called in the others and asked them each to take on an additional class until he found a replacement. They all agreed except Bodger. "I like teaching," Bodger said. "But taking on extra work without pay wouldn't be fair to my wife."

The remaining unassigned class was taken by Stokes.

"Next time, find a nice ordinary family guy," Stokes said. "Sure, I'll teach the class. What is it? Letter Writing? I know how to write letters."

"It's called 'Communications Theory.'"

"Then I can bullshit all I want. Is there a text?"

"Yes. Are you sure this is your field, Clem?"

Stokes smiled. "I can teach anything except scuba diving. What's the schedule?"

A week later, by design, Wiliam strolled past the windows of the classroom Stokes was teaching in. Thirty grinning students were facing the podium where another student was delivering a talk. Stokes was at the back with his feet on the table in front of him. William hung about the corridor and put himself in the way of one of the students who had come to see him. In response to his elaborately casual question, the student volunteered the information that the Communications Theory class was now his best class, and that Dr. Stokes was the best teacher he had ever had.

At his weekly meeting, Stokes said, "Communications Theory is all right, but I'd sooner teach Philosophy. By the way, can I have a word with you, William?" He nodded to dismiss the other chairmen. When they were alone, he said, "There was a guy in here the other day warning me about you. Welsh guy, big, greasy. Said you were a con man, your credentials were phony."

"What did you say?"

"I thanked him. Then I phoned your references. They seem okay. What's he got against you?"

"I refused to hire him."

"That all?" Stokes looked at him thoughtfully, then shrugged. "Let's hope it's just me he's talking to."

xii. If Winter Comes

A FEW DAYS later a replacement for Penzler was found and the term settled down.

William found the chairman's job wholly absorbing. Much of his time was spent just listening. Once or twice a day students sought his advice, or appealed to his authority or, occasionally, registered a complaint. After Penzler, the complaints seemed trivial and he resolved them easily. Two or three times a week students consulted him on non-academic matters. As a chairman, he automatically made the list of people polled by student reporters about topics such as whether students should be forced to wear ties.

He was on six committees in his official capacity and was elected to three others. Some of the committees met regularly, the committee which dealt with complaints about the food in the cafeteria, for example, and some only once or twice a year, like the Awards Committee, which met to decide who should get the President's Gold Medal, awarded partly on marks, but also on effort, contribution to student life, and even, occasionally, deportment.

All of which made his day full, sometimes interesting, and much less strenuous than teaching.

In mid-term the institute closed for half a day for the Annual Winter Carnival. A dozen large blocks of ice were delivered to a bit of waste ground behind the Bible College, and competing groups of students hacked them into shapes. Nine of the twelve blocks were sculpted into the shape of female nudes. One, destroyed immediately on the orders of the police, was dedicated to Priapus. One was an attempt at technology's greatest triumph, the wheel. The last, in charge of R. Brown, was left untouched. Brown planned to photograph it at intervals as it melted, and thus create a work of art by mounting the resulting series of pictures. Brown said, "The real work will, of course, consist of the changing shape of the mass of ice in *time*. All my camera can do is freeze some moments in the flux, as if a photographer found his true subject in Botticelli's *Primavera* rather than spring itself."

On the day of the carnival, before the judging could begin, the weather broke and the skies poured with rain. By the afternoon, all of the sculptures had lost their identity, creating a fiasco for everyone, except Brown, who clicked away happily recording and creating art.

At R. Brown's urging, William continued to teach one class a week, and here, too, he found some prestige from his new title spilling into the classroom. R. Brown asked, "Is it still 'Mr.,' sir? It hardly seems adequate."

His private life was uneventful and flawless. He now lived in a small attic flat within walking distance of the institute, and he took his major meals out. His salary had more than doubled and he was thus rich by any standard, having more money than he could spend. When he wanted diversion he talked to Geoffrey Spindle, or listened to Mordecai Redburn, or made love to Jane. On Saturdays he walked all day, from bookshop to bookshop, and on Sundays he read *The New York Times*, which took all day. He was very content.

There was a slightly heavy feeling about February. Everyone remarked on it. And then it was March, and the term began racing to a conclusion. The approach of spring was signalled by the annual meeting of the Faculty Association. The president of the association reported to the meeting that he was still negotiating the terms under which the association would support the president's bid for independence. He received a vote of thanks and a mandate to continue to act as he thought fit. Everyone was eager to get on with the party that always followed the meeting.

Garbage cans full of beer and ice were unveiled, and huge enamel bowls of chili con carne, and cabbage soaked in mayonnaise, and bread. Everyone lined up and spooned the food on to cardboard plates. Spindle said, "Cunningham wants to call this room the 'Refectory.' I think he feels that silver and white napery will follow. He's asked me to work out a bit of Latin to go round the walls — he remembers seeing it somewhere, and thought it a nice touch. I suggested we break fresh ground, not hanker after stale learning, but use something from one of the early Canadian explorers. My own favourite for a dining room would be the bit in Champlain's diary where he talks about how they were kept awake at night by the noise of the salmon jumping in the Saint Clair River. Sit tight now; it looks as if 'seconds' are to be announced, so hold on to the edge of the table until they've gone by."

Seconds *were* announced, and Spindle and William clung to their table as it was banged from both sides by the tide of diners running to refill their plates. Afterward, the maintenance staff swept up the food that had fallen on the floor, a space was cleared, and the dancing began. An hour passed sedately enough, then two hours disappeared, and it was ten o'clock, and the room was full of teachers — shouting, leaping, and occasionally falling.

Maisie Clipsham sought him out. She smelled of hot lavender, and there was a hint of perspiration on her upper lip. "Would you dance with me?" she yelled into his ear. He stood up and moved to take her into a formal embrace, but she shook him off and stationed herself with a yard between them, and started to jiggle. "I like the new dancing," she said. "You don't get covered in sweaty hands." He took the hint and jiggled at a distance. But after four bottles of beer he was unreserved. "Maisie," he shouted. "I think you care too much about being sweaty. The world has to smell of something."

"You think I have a fetish," she screamed, smiling.

"Yes, I do, a bit. Not much. Just a bit."

"What should I do about it?"

"Try to resist the temptation to scrub up all the time."

"All right. Let's go home to your place. Sleep in our underwear. In your filthy sheets. Get laid in the morning before we've brushed our teeth. Eat breakfast stinking of sex."

"Maisie, you're drunk."

"I mean it."

"All right. I must dance with the president's wife, then I'll come and find you."

"I'll go and work up a sweat with the Bodger." She jiggled off, fierce and determined.

The music increased in volume, but the style changed as those teachers one generation from their rural roots became sufficiently relaxed to demand their favourites. One or two modest cowboy yells were heard and the party moved into its final phase as the polkas began.

William danced with Jane and explained that he would not be seeing her afterward. It was not their regular night, but he was afraid that she might be assuming that it was an exception. She was surprised — she *had* rather thought they would make a night of it — but sanguine, confirming that he could join her two nights hence. Mordecai hung around at the end. "Will you be taking some woman home?" he asked.

"I hope so," William said. "I feel horny."

This was pointed enough, and Mordecai sagged in despair. "I thought perhaps I might come home with you. We could have some cocoa together. Play a game of Monopoly. If you *weren't* taking some woman home."

"No. I'm busy tonight."

"Ah." Mordecai slumped sadly in his chair.

The president and his wife appeared, slowly circling the dining room. "This is very nice," he said, "but we should try for something a bit more formal. Don't you agree, Jocasta?"

"There are several teachers dancing in suspenders, Gravely. I think they're teachers. If they're not, it doesn't matter."

"Not my place to interfere, dear. We are guests here. Besides, it might be fashionable. We don't go out much."

When they had passed by, William shook off Mordecai and went in search of Maisie, who had said she would wait for him to find her. But Maisie was gone. William hung about for half an hour, then walked over to Jane's flat, but her light was already out.

Next day Maisie said, "Sorry about last night. I don't know what came over me."

"Did you get sick?"

"No. I mean, talking like that."

"I was flattered," he said gallantly.

xiii. Meanwhile,
Up at the Buildings . . .

THE MINISTER RESPONSIBLE for Van Horne was talking to his deputy. "Mary Jane has tried everything else. Now she's heard of this Van Horne place where she can study wall-paper design or some such bullshit. Do they really teach that kind of thing there?"

"It's called 'Design Studies,' I believe, sir, but it has its applied side."

"Can you get her in?"

"No difficulty about that. But are you sure? I don't think she'll find many friends there."

"Mary Jane is twenty-three. It's time she was off my hands. Maybe a spell at this Van Horne place will do her good. I went down the mine when I was fifteen. Had my first woman that pay-day. Now tell me something about this place. Is it ours? Mine? Am I responsible for it? How come we haven't had any trouble from the students?"

The deputy minister sighed. All this had been included in the minister's briefing, six weeks before, when he had been switched away from the Recreational Living portfolio so that two motels he owned in cottage country could qualify for building grants. The minister was a coming man, everybody said so, but there had been four ministers in the job in less than a year and the deputy was tired of teaching them. But their ignorance was his to use.

"Van Horne is the baby of the system," he began. "But it may be the prototype for the future. At the moment it is unique, but practical education is becoming fashionable again. I think it might be the kind of institute that the Ministry could focus on for the future."

The minister started to reply, then put his hands behind his head and leaned back. "Sit down, Percy," he said, "and tell me what you're up to."

"Nothing yet, minister. But I do foresee that Van Horne could be important in an era of change."

"Do you? An era of change, eh? I like the sound of that. I'll write that down. What's in it for you?"

"I think it might be an opportunity for us to take a real part in post-secondary education, sir. Van Horne belongs to the department, us. There isn't even any enabling legislation, let alone a charter, whereas the universities are entirely auton-omous under the Act."

"Uh-huh. The Council of University Presidents have been pissing on you, eh?"

"They do tend to stress their independence whenever we offer to help."

"Don't they, though? So what's our line?"

"We must educate for change. The times require a greater flexibility of response than the traditional institutions allow. Look at your daughter, a typical member of today's youth."

"Let's leave her out of it. I like the rest of it, though. 'Educate for change.' Yes, that's very nice. Put that in my speech for when I get that honorary degree. I'll remember that for when I have to speak off the cuff, as well. What's our first move?"

"What we need is an assistant to me with special responsibility for technical education. That would symbolize the importance the government places on it."

"And on you, eh, Percy? Got someone in mind?"

"I've had some thoughts about the kind of person we want."

"I bet you have. Who?"

"Could I nail him down first, if I have your approval to go ahead? I'd like to float the idea, send up a trial balloon."

"All right, have your fun. When do I start dropping hints to the press?"

"You might speculate, informally, just an idea you've been playing with. First to the *Keyhole*, that Ottawa rag. We owe them something for keeping quiet about your uncle in that Mexican resort. I'll suggest it's time they requested an interview with you. Late in the day. If you're tired you could take him out to dinner."

"You do enjoy this insider stuff, don't you? All right, then. Maybe I'll mention Mary Jane, something about how I've been talking to my daughter lately who's not interested in university but wants to train for life. By studying wallpaper at Van Horne. And this has made me realize that there are probably a lot like her in that generation, that we must listen to them and not impose out-of-date assumptions in an era of change. That the wisdom of the young . . ."

"That's exactly the right note, sir," the deputy said, cutting in quickly.

" . . . babes and sucklings," the minister finished. "One thing, Percy. You won't get too deep into this, will you? I mean, have your fun, but don't forget the leadership convention's only six weeks away."

"I think the timing's just right, sir."

"You plan for us to make Van Horne a plank, like? In my leadership platform?"

"It fits."

"And what do you get out of it?"

"Satisfaction, sir."

"Spare me the bullshit, Percy. But I can wait."

Two days later the Bible College was abuzz. The column in the *Keyhole* had been distributed among the faculty. Gravely Cunningham said to Clem Stokes, "This is the first time I've ever been mentioned in the press, Clem. Very encouraging. Who do you think the minister will get for this new job, the assistant deputy responsible for technical education?"

"One of his own boys, I should think. An instructor from the School of Mines, I shouldn't wonder. It's in his riding."

"But the administration of technological education would involve far more than mining. He'll have to find someone with a wide knowledge of the field."

"He won't get an American or an Englishman. The *Keyhole* wouldn't stand for that. Not any more."

The chairman of Design Studies hunted feverishly through his files. "Here it is." He waved a form in the air. "Mary Jane Tupper. Rejected. Jesus Christ. Here." He tore the words "Not Approved" from the bottom of the form and taped on a fresh bit of paper, stamping it with a flourish, "Approved." "Photocopy it so the tear looks like a crease, then send it registered mail," he said to the girl who did the department's typing.

That afternoon the deputy minister entertained a visitor about the new appointment. "All set, Clem." He rubbed his hands. "When could you start?"

"I could use a bit of a holiday. Say in three weeks?"

"Fine. Salary all right? What about a car?"

"I'll leave all that to you, Percy."

"Sorry it's a bit sudden. I thought when we talked last year that it would be another couple of months. But the timing's right."

"I've been ready for a while. I'll hear from Gravely then that you want to approach me? He was asking me this morning who I thought might get the job."

"Probably early in the week. I'm glad you're coming, Clem. We'll have some fun."

"What's it *really* all about, Percy? What are you up to?"

"I think Van Horne's on the move, and I need someone in the office here to keep an eye on it, someone who knows how the place works, and who to watch for."

"Gravely's very ambitious. You know that."

"I got that impression. Still, that's not a fault, is it?"

"I'd have thought you might have found it a nuisance."

"Not necessarily. I've been telling the minister, we have to educate for change. That's what Van Horne is all about."

"You mean we'll be encouraging Gravely? I thought you might want me to contain him a bit."

"Up to a point, Percy. Let's hear what he has to say."

"I see," Stokes, who was beginning to, said. "You'll let me know when we've got to that point, will you?"

The deputy minister picked a letter off his desk. "By the way, one of your people has recommended herself for the job I want you for. Know her? Jane Goray?"

"Sure." Stokes picked up the letter. "She must have her ear to the ground. I wonder where she gets her information?"

"She's marked her application 'strictly confidential.' What else is she up to? I'll keep her on file, shall I?"

"Oh, yes, let's keep an eye on her."

II
Snakes,
and Ladders

i. Excelsior

THE PRESIDENT CALLED William into his office a week
later. "Moodie, how would you like to be Director of
Humane Studies?"

"But I've only just got going as chairman, sir. Besides, what
about Mr. Stokes. Has he been fired?"

The president looked irritated. "A word to the wise,
Moodie. When someone offers you a job, don't ask him what
happened to the last man. As a matter of fact, Clem has
resigned. The minister has offered him a job in the Buildings.
He's deserted us, Moodie, but we'd all do the same. In the
meantime, it's the last day of term, and I need a Director of
Humane Studies."

"What about Pardoe, sir? The chairman of Related Studies?"

"Another word of advice. When someone offers you a job,
assume you are the first choice. But as a matter of information,
I'm thinking of Pardoe for the job of Registrar."

"But we don't have a registrar."

"We ought to, don't you think? Everyone else has a registrar. I think Pardoe would be ideal. Now, what about a replacement for you. Who is there?"

"Mordecai Redburn."

"Dear God."

"Geoffrey Spindle."

"He'd refuse."

"Jack Bodger."

"Is he the one who tried to sell me a lottery ticket? No."

"Then there's just Maisie Clipsham or the new man, Chubb." William thought about it. Why not. "I recommend Maisie. It's time for a woman chairman in the division."

"You're the one who has to work with her. If she's agreeable, go ahead. Will you approach her today? That would cut down on the speculation about your present job when people hear about you."

"I'll do it now."

"Just one thing, Moodie. Incidentally, Stokes and I used first names. Mine is Gravely. Yours is William? All right, William, I had a telephone call from the police the other day. The head of the morality squad said you had been 'found in' at a raid on an after-hours drinking club. He isn't going to press charges, but he thought I ought to know. I hope this isn't a habit. I don't want my directors in the courts."

"It isn't true, Gravely. I've never been arrested."

"Why would the police make up a thing like that?"

"I don't think it was the police. Did he have a Welsh accent?"

"Yes, he did, now that you mention it. Someone you know? A joke?"

"Sort of."

"Odd friends you've got. Keep them under control, if you can."

Maisie snapped the job up. The announcements were made and William, as director, held his first meeting of the division's administrators on the last day of term. Pardoe had accepted the job of registrar, and a new chairman of his department had yet to be appointed, so William and Maisie chatted for half an hour and went their separate ways, thinking of their new salaries.

William's way took him on a tour of the maritime provinces with Jane, who was herself now a chairman of the Department of Personal Design. They made love in New Brunswick bed-and-breakfasts and were assumed to be on their honeymoon (in those days Jane wore a ring on their overnight stays in the Maritimes), and in Quebec *auberges,* where they were assumed to be adulterers; moved on to Prince Edward Island, where they stayed for a week in a farmhouse in Tignish, eating lobsters and strawberries, and avoiding the places, like Lucy Maud Montgomery's house, where they might be seen by other tourists. From the Island they drove down through the Maine woods and turned west for home.

"Things are going well for you, aren't they?" she said one night in a motel in upstate New York. "Do you think it's because you are extraordinary?"

"No, but I believe I'm on a progress, moving towards some kind of climax. I have no sense that I'm in control. Ever since I was sent to Van Horne, which I'd never heard of, I've been on the move. Things are happening which will go on happening until I find out what it's all about, whatever 'it' is. And when it stops, I won't be able to do anything about that, either."

"You people always get so mystical about it. I thought literature and philosophy were supposed to make you critical and sceptical."

"I am. Both of those. I don't believe in God or luck or anything like that. But that doesn't stop me from feeling like a pawn that someone is making into a king."

"There you go again. Could we stop talking for a bit? By the way, I'll drop you off on the American side of Niagara Falls, at the bus station. We might run into someone we know across the bridge."

Mordecai sought him out as soon as the new term started. There was a considerable change in his appearance. The standard Canadian costume of blue blazer and grey flannels, lightly touched up of late with a *boutonnière*, was gone. In its place, Mordecai had on a pair of blue jeans and a huge grey sweatshirt. His black oxfords had been replaced by tennis shoes.

William agreed to have supper with him, adding, "I don't know what's been happening to you, but you seem to be in a different world from when I last saw you. And different from me, too."

"Not so different. That Jane Goray is a bit old for me, but I wouldn't mind trying her. They say experience makes up for a lack of bloom. That the case?" He watched William closely for his reaction.

William said, "Let's have dinner Thursday night. How did you know about Jane?"

Mordecai said, "I guessed. You are so casual when you are together in public that you look like a couple of spies passing messages and worrying about hidden cameras. It wasn't hard for a jealous lad to figure out."

At dinner, Mordecai said, "I'm a tit man myself. Is that right?"

"It depends. What are you trying to say?"

"I mean I'm turned on by the mammaries, not the *derrière*."

"Then you have the right phrase. May I ask — any particular ones?"

"Sure you may. Right now I'm balling a chick in Health Sciences, the assistant chairman. I screw a girl in my building on Sunday nights. And then there's my dentist's receptionist."

"Three!"

"Two plus. I haven't actually had the receptionist yet." Mordecai relapsed into his former idiom. "Not so much, really, is it? For someone like you, it must seem a low score."

"Not to me. Not everybody is as interested in sex as you now seem to be."

"Don't get stuffy with me, old boy. I had no idea. You're right: I think about it all the time. You see that chick over there? I'd like to . . ."

"Yes, yes. When did all this happen? Three weeks ago you had a very different orientation."

"You were right. Three weeks ago I was a lonely adolescent, with you as my only chum. My shrink says now that he thinks I was going through the pre-adolescent same-sex bonding stage, when all one's energy is focused on a close friend."

"That's all in the past, is it?"

"After my last session on the couch I became aware of some kind of change. The nature of it didn't become clear until later. I was in the apartment of a lady I know and I told her something of my condition. She was interested and asked me if I had ever tried to focus my desires. I said, no, but as a matter of fact the question had just arisen, and she offered to help."

"And it worked?"

"Oh, yeah. She was very considerate. I'll always be grateful. She led me through, step by step. First — do you want to hear all this? You must remember your first time?"

"Yes. Every experience is different. Tell me."

"Well, first we had a bath together, a real scrub-up from head to toe, and everywhere else, and then she arranged the scene — perfumed sheets, the whole bit. I've since found out that a good greasy piece has its own pleasures, but she was right for a first time. My shrink now says it was a classsical initiation of the young male by an older woman." He passed a hand modestly through his bright grey hair.

"My God. How old was she?"

"What? Oh, I see. Well, in ordinary terms, about thirty, I think, but remember I'm really . . ."

"Yes, yes, I see. Mordecai, was it Maisie?"

"I think guys who brag about their women, naming names, are cruddy, but you're right. I've never been back. I don't know if she wants me to."

"What a nice thing for her to do, though."

"It wasn't all one-sided, old boy." Mordecai was defensive and proud.

"No, I'm sure. And now you're insatiable."

"Now I'm irresistible. Women know when you're getting it and they all want some. I'm surrounded by crooked fingers in doorways, as it were. I can see how one might get tired. You must be whacked out."

"The next thing to learn, Mordecai, is that no two people are alike. And don't ask me how often I do it. That's how adolescents talk, and you're out of that stage."

"You mean that you, everybody, isn't shagging all the time?" Mordecai was amazed. "But you don't mind if I share my experience with you? I don't think I'm quite in the final stage yet."

"No, no. Tell me all. Just don't assume I'm your twin. And another thing. Gossiping is as bad as bragging. I'd like your promise that you will never breathe a word to anyone about me and Jane."

"Why the anxiety?"

"It would do irreparable harm if it got out."

"You'd have to go back to teaching, you mean?"

"No. Not socially or politically. Personally. She would cut me off."

Mordecai looked thoughtful. "Why? I see. She gets her jollies by having you in secret, right? I must ask my shrink how typical that is. You know it sounds to me . . ."

William let him ramble on. The danger seemed to be contained for the moment.

ii. Meanwhile . . .

WHEN HE WAS settled behind his desk, his coffee in front of him, the minister said, "I think I know what's going on now, Percy. I went fishing on Sunday; between bites I worked out what you are up to. Sit down and listen to what I think." He held out his hand to tick off the fingers. "One, you think that the times are changing and there'll be a shortage of students soon, right?"

"More or less." The deputy minister watched his boss's hand.

"Two. But with your help Van Horne could turn this into an opportunity."

"More or less."

"Three. Perhaps grow while the others shrink a bit, screaming their fucking heads off."

"Yes."

"Four. But what happens to Van Horne, if it's good, happens to you and me, because it still belongs to us, whereas if we give these other guys the moon they'll still piss on us. Right?"

"Yes."

"And if Cunningham's little institute grows, we could get the credit, because we could be seen to be directing the scarce taxpayers' money into practical stuff. Right?"

"I think that's how it would come out."

"So do I. What number am I up to? Five? And all this will happen in time for the leadership convention, will it?"

"The news of it, yes. But there is a practical matter of tactics at the convention itself. Can you spare half an hour?"

"Take all the time you want."

The division ran itself without interference from William. Once a week the two chairmen met in his office to review their problems. This took about an hour. Apart from this, William's job was to combine the work of the two departments into a single divisional set of numbers and statements. This took a day. Much of the rest of his time was spent in activities that existed only because his office existed. Visitors to the institute were introduced to him, sometimes over lunches that took two hours. A great deal of casual mail was directed to him, some of it redirected from the president's office. All of this had to be read because periodically it contained an invitation to spend time at another organization's expense. In his first month William spent two days in New York looking at computers, and four days in southern California being introduced to the latest concept in language laboratories.

His major personal contribution was to listen to the president dream of the Van Horne of the future. They met on Mondays for lunch in the president's office, and talked through the afternoon.

"It's largely a matter of labels," Cunningham said at the first of these meetings. "We can do anything we like if we get the labels right." He looked out of the window of his office, nodding gently.

William, watching his gaze, guessed that instead of the photographic supplies shop opposite, the president was seeing the new, as yet unplanned, laboratory buildings. Instead of the house with the derelicts drinking wine on the steps, he saw the new student residence. Everywhere he looked, instead of the urban blight that had made the original site of the institute so cheap, he saw the graceful towers, grass surroundings, and gravel paths of the City Technical University.

"Here's an example," the president continued. "I propose that henceforth you fellows be called 'deans.' Most places have deans nowadays. Sound the others out to see if there's any problem. Now what else? What else does a college have? A proper college."

"A library?"

"We've got one of sorts, haven't we? In the corner room of the Drug Mart."

"Just a few shelves, Gravely. Not many of the faculty know about it. It ought to have some standard reference works. Encyclopedias, things like that."

"We can afford a couple of thousand from the cleaning budget. Draw up a list. But now you've mentioned it, what is the real mark of a library?"

"Other than books?"

"Yes. What else?"

"A copying machine?"

"What else?"

It was important to guess right. Cunningham was getting impatient. "I am not sure of your emphasis, Gravely," he hedged.

"Emphasis? How do you know it *is* a library?"

"The sign on the door?"

"Exactly. The label, William, the label. Get a sign made. And what do people find inside the door?"

"The librarian?"

"Now you're on to it. Apart from the sign, the cheapest thing in the library is the librarian, especially since they aren't unionized. We could put anyone in and call him the librarian. Now who have we got?"

"Beckett?"

Beckett was a religious maniac, a clerk in the maintenance department who spent his lunch-hours walking the streets with a billboard, warning of the end. His fellow workers complained constantly about his proselytizing in the storeroom.

"Perfect. He's a bit more eccentric than most librarians, I suppose, but he'll do. Is he conscientious?"

"It's the other thing his colleagues dislike about him."

"Done, then. Now we have deans and a librarian. What else?"

But they were interrupted by the secretary with the announcement that a visitor had arrived to keep an appointment with the president.

The next week they met again and picked up the topic immediately.

"I've made a list, Gravely," William said, as soon as they had finished their lunch. "We need a bursar, a registrar, a dean's list of good students, some essay prizes, a buttery, a refectory, a chapel, squash courts, an orchestra, and some campus police."

"Wonderfully well done. Let's see: we'll make Miss Scrivener the bursar — she's the cashier, she'll like that. A registrar we have, though Pardoe wants to call himself Director of Student Affairs or some such rubbish. He thinks the model ought to be Texas Technical Institute. No chapel, I think. Squash courts? The shed behind the Drug Mart. Campus police is *very* good; we'll buy Hans at the gate a new uniform with a name patch. I'll have my secretary go to work on all this right away. You've missed one thing, though."

"Gothic arches?"

"Try again."

"A bell tower?"

"We'll get a record player. One more try." Cunningham was in an agony of excitement, his head nodding as if on a spring.

"You'll have to tell me, Gravely. I can't think."

"A board of governors, William. *A board of governors!*"

"But wouldn't a board of governors interfere a bit? Tell you what to do?"

"The board I have in mind would be purely nominal. Their job will be to raise money for us and sit on the platform at convocation."

"I see. It's the idea that matters, not the people."

"Exactly. Now we are still a bit short on tradition. I was thinking of our graduation ceremony. At Oxford, you know, they hit you on the head with a bible. I watched it once when I was living nearby. I wonder if we could kill two birds with one stone. We can't hit students with a bible, too many Jews and whatnot, but I thought we might carry a bible in the procession, and here's why. In a sense we are the inheritors of the old Bible College, and I was wondering if they might be persuaded to give us a bible to which some historical significance attached, and we could explain it in a little note in the program." He looked slyly at William. "Then, you see, if the Bible College were pleased, they might ante up a scholarship, even sponsor a joint course of study."

"A Dip. Tech. in Theology?"

"No, no. A one-term course in Comparative Religion, or 'The Bible as Literature.' Surely we could do something like that?"

"Who would take it?"

"The problem is whom do we have to help *give* it."

William thought. "There are two people, a rabbi and a former monk. Both of them teach interpersonal relationships in the Commercial Studies program. Shopsy also teaches philosophy on the side."

"Splendid. Sound them out, would you?"

And so it came about that Lonny Shopsy and Sean O'Sullivan each undertook to teach half of a half-course in Religious Values. Shopsy did the Old Testament, and O'Sullivan took the new. It was described in the calendar as offered "By Arrangement with the former Bible College," which provided, directly, the money for that portion of the instructors' salaries.

That night, Jane said, "Dean, eh. Sounds a bit grand. You'll be leaving me behind."

"Rubbish. But while we are on the subject, Mordecai Redburn knows all about us."

"What?" She pushed him off. "What does he know?"

"About us. He watched us, and guessed."

"Why?"

"He was lonely, and jealous, I think."

"Shit."

"Not to worry. He won't tell anybody. It's all right."

"It's not all right. That's it for us."

"I promise you Mordecai can be trusted. He's not interested in us any more. He's too busy now with his own life."

After a few moments she said, "If you're sure. But don't come near here in daylight. Understand?"

Later on, much calmer, she said, "I sometimes think I'm bored by everything about men except this."

"Even me?"

"I'm afraid so. Never mind. There will always be this."

iii. A Board of Governors

TWO DAYS LATER the deputy minister found the opportunity to talk to his superior.

"They still want to piss on Van Horne, do they?" the minister asked. "What do they have in mind? Make the students wear coveralls and hard hats? Do they know Mary Jane is a student there?"

"I wouldn't think so. The point is, they're afraid that times will get rough and Van Horne will be competing with them for students."

"So they want to put Cunningham on a leash, do they? Careful, Percy. Some of these presidents play rough."

"I think we want to seem to tie your hands in public, as far as they are concerned, and at the same time make it hard for Cunningham to do anything we don't want. Let Van Horne seem independent and still keep it under control."

"That sounds nice." The minister looked at his watch. "How have you arranged to do that?"

"I thought if we gave Van Horne a board of governors, we could keep them both quiet."

"There's a flaw, Percy. I'm surprised at you. If Van Horne had a board of governors, it really would be independent."

"It will be your board, sir. You will appoint them."

"Right. Aren't I the dumb bunny?" The minister had his coat on and was pouring himself a small whisky. "And who will they be?"

"I thought Wesley Basingstoke, Hargreaves — one or two like that."

"Not too thick. A couple of old hands will be enough. Don't forget to add one or two on their way up. One Italian, at least."

"No problem. Shall I start talking to Cunningham, then?"

The minister made for the door. "I'll tell you what, Percy. These things can get away from you. Put yourself on, too, okay."

"Oh, yes. You *have* to have your representative on. Yes, I'd taken that for granted."

"I have broached the matter in the broadest possible terms, Gravely, but you must leave it with me now. Giving you a board of governors is likely to alarm the Council of Presidents. They think you are getting above yourself as it is, with all this talk of deans and professors. Frankly, they'd like to squash you. They are afraid of what you would do next. Degrees?" The deputy minister laughed and sucked the meat from a crab leg.

They were lunching in the Glass Pavilion, a fashionable restaurant created out of the shell of an old sailors' mission.

"But it will happen, won't it?" Cunningham pleaded.

"I can't guarantee anything, but the minister is pleased with what you've done with Van Horne."

"His daughter likes it," Cunningham said eagerly.

The deputy minister winced and sipped his wine. "Even in the farming constituencies, the minister would have to lean over backwards *not* to show favour on that account. Politics is not as crude as that."

"But it *will* happen?" Cunningham repeated, humbly now.

"Leave it in my hands. But first, not a word to anyone. The idea will have to come from us, or seem to."

A thought occurred to Cunningham. "Why should you and the minister want this?"

"We are fond of Van Horne, Gravely. Besides, the minister doesn't want the Council of Presidents to think they can tell him what to do about Van Horne, not now his . . . that is, in this day and age." He winked. "And now I must go. Would you mind paying for this? The auditor general is looking at the accounts this month, and I noticed this morning your expenses have been negligible."

"I never go out."

"As I understand it, it's because the minister likes us." Cunningham beamed at the president of the Faculty Association.

"Oh, yeah? Great. Now, sir, I think the Faculty Association will agree with the new status under the terms we discussed."

"Draw up the terms and have William here go over them, and have the agreement ready." Cunningham was hardly listening.

Back in his office, William asked, "Who will be eligible for membership in the Faculty Association?"

"All members of the faculty except the president. Lonny Shopsy says we have to leave him out so as to have someone to bargain with."

"The librarian?"

"Beckett? Oh no. He hasn't got a degree. You have to have a proper degree to belong to the association."

"That seems all right then. Let's sign it, shall we, and have a drink on it."

iv. Student Unrest

NOTHING HAPPENED FOR two months, while Cunningham waited for news in his office. William now spent about three days a week with the president, talking about the future and watching the routine work of the office move across his desk, untouched, into the OUT tray, whence the secretary brought it to William in his office.

"I wish they'd get on with it." Cunningham's voice was full of longing.

To fill in time he appointed William Vice President Academic. "All the other colleges have them," he said. "I don't think we can spare any of the other deans."

There were two developments. The Dean of Consumer Studies, a cabinet-maker by profession, resigned in a temper to return to teaching. He did not wish, he said, to work for some young asshole who knew nothing from nothing except about story books. Next thing, he said, they would all be teaching *Winnie-the-*goddamn*-Pooh*.

William set up a search committee to find a new Dean of Consumer Studies, and from the list of names they offered him, selected Jane. "It's time we had a woman as dean," he told the committee.

His other problem was to find a new Dean of Arts. This time the committee offered him a list including Maisie, whom he appointed.

Jane said, "If everyone knew we were having it off, you couldn't have made me dean, could you? Now do you understand?"

Spindle said, "You realize what is happening? This new young chairman of ours is more qualified academically than you are. And he's Canadian. In other words, even the people who know all about us want to come here. We are becoming respectable." He bit off a thread and smoothed out the square he was working on.

William sipped his beer and looked up from the book of *New Yorker* cartoons he had found in Geoffrey's bookcase. "You think so? Most of the students still seem like late bloomers."

"But not all. I had a man in my class this week who knew the proper origin of the possessive apostrophe. Do you know?"

"Certainly. The 's' is short for 'his,' as in, 'John his book.'"

"Yes, it's a flaw in your education, too. Actually the apostrophe is formed from the old genetive as it existed when the noun was inflected. This lad knew this. Picked it up somewhere."

"But we've always had the odd R. Brown."

"This one is different. He's not eccentric, he just knows more than they used to. We're beginning to attract students."

"Do you think Cunningham is right? You know, 'Assume a virtue if you have it not and you'll soon acquire it.'"

"Pass me that bit of orange calico, would you? No, that's beige silk. Calico. That's it. Thank you. No doubt of it. If it happens quickly enough, I might become mainstream again."

They both laughed heartily.

One day R. Brown came to see him in his new capacity of president of the student union. "I wanted to tell you that we are preparing an anti-calendar," he said. "You don't teach any more so you won't have to worry. We have decided not to be scientific. In my view, all those careful questionnaires designed to eliminate bias are hokum. Bias is the name of the game. Human beings are infinitely various and not capable of being reduced to a set of characteristics. They are capable of being judged, though, by other human beings as various as they are. The judgements are indefensible in the sense that they are formed subconsciously as the result of factors unknown to the judge himself, thousands of messages received over the course of the year. So I have designed a form which asks the student to rate the instructor on a scale from one to ten, based on hunch and prejudice. Make no attempt to justify your choice. You see? Finally, one single judgement. Ten out of ten will mean the student thinks you are terrific; at the other end, if you score zero, it means you are an absolute tit. The joy of it is that the students will know it is totally accurate, but the Faculty Association can deny its validity. The first evaluation that is invalid but true. In tests so far it has worked perfectly."

Up at the Buildings, the minister said, "Aren't you about ready, Percy? There isn't much time to move without looking obvious. I need something to keep my name in lights, but I don't want it to look like a leadership ploy already."

"I'm just about ready. We need an emergency, something that will force us to go ahead. I have an idea."

"Don't tell me. As Pockett is always saying, 'Never let them tell you where the money comes from.'"

"Keep next Thursday free."

That afternoon, Percy's assistant, Clem Stokes, telephoned Klopstock, the president of the Faculty Association. The two men discussed labour relations, and the next day Klopstock cornered the president of the student union and took him for a corned beef sandwich.

R. Brown said, "This is my first smoky back room." He rubbed his hands excitedly.

Half an hour later he was capering in his seat with glee. "So this is how it works. You want me to lean on the Buildings, right? But they know it's coming, right? In fact, it's *the Buildings* that want me to lean on them, right?" R. Brown made his eyes into slits, negating the effect with a giant smile.

"All I said was . . .," Klopstock began.

R. Brown leaned over and patted Klopstock's hand. "No need to retract your balls, old son. Trust me. I can feel an idea forming already. Stay by the phone." He went off chuckling.

Two days later the troubles, labelled "The Independence Riots" in the student newspaper, began.

v. Autres moeurs

ON FRIDAY MORNING two African students were informed by their department that they had failed the physical education requirement because they had not participated in the required number of classes. This meant they would lose their year and return to their homelands in disgrace.

The two students were perfectly willing to attend classes. Both of them were superb athletes who revelled in every kind of sport. Though they preferred soccer to any of the games available, they were quite prepared to play anything required. They refused, however, to shower with the rest of the class, asking instead to be allowed to wash in private. They said they found the idea of trying to cleanse themselves in a pool of filth, draining off the bodies around them, revolting. But there were no private showers, and it was a rule that no one was allowed to finish a Physical Education class without showering.

No one said anything at the beginning as they absented themselves from class and practised heading a ball up and down the corridor outside the gym, so the Africans assumed the institute was turning a blind eye. Even when they received their notices, they were not concerned, assuming still that someone had not told everybody about them. But when they went to see the chairman of their department they were surprised to be told that they must observe the forms. (After they left, the chairman phoned Klopstock. "I hope this turns out all right. I could look very bad."

"We all could, " Klopstock said. "But R. Brown seems to know what he's doing. What started this, anyway? Some cultural taboo?"

"I think they're just shy.")

The two Africans were not encouraged to see the dean, the chairman making it clear that everyone above would support him. Either they repeat the year (it was now too late to catch up on the physical education requirement separately) or they would be asked to leave. The chairman said, off the record, that if he were they, he would try to get help from the president of the student union.

R. Brown was waiting for them, had been waiting all morning. He heard them out, his face registering the emotions of horror, anger, and disgust. "Please wait," he said, when they had finished their tale. "George, Dmitri, come in here for a minute."

Two members of his executive joined the group and heard the story again, duplicated R. Brown's reaction, and supplied the first crowd response.

R. Brown picked up the telephone, and dialled a number. "Student union here. I have two students in my office who say you are forcing them to violate the customs of their culture, to the point of asking them to offend against religious proscriptions. What? Oh, yes. Many cultures derive their cleansing as well as dietary rules from their religions. What? Well, Jews, for example. No, these guys aren't Jews — you aren't, are you? — I was speaking by way of analogy. What? Oh, Christ then. Let me put it simply: you are making them wash in public, which they don't like. No. It isn't up to you and me to tell the world how to behave, is it? The point is, do you stand by your order? You must? You have no choice? Right." R. Brown put down the phone and turned to the students. "When is your next Physical Education class? Tomorrow? Turn up for it. We shall be there."

The next day, Brown addressed the class as they waited for the Physical Education instructor to arrive. The two Africans stood beside him. "It is a question of individual rights," he told the crowd. "If they can make Winston and Benjamin commit practices abhorrent to them, they will feel free to make us all hew to the culture of whoever is in charge of Physical Education. But Canada is a mosaic, not a melting pot. We must preserve the right to wash as we please."

The Africans were popular with the other students, and the crowd needed little urging.

"Down with the Physical Education department," a Chinese student shouted.

R. Brown held up his hand. "Now, if you are willing, I propose that we boycott Physical Education until Winston and Benjamin are allowed to shower in private."

That night Brown telephoned the press, and the next day pictures of the empty gym appeared in one of the papers with the headline "Naked Students Forced to Parade in Public."

Two more classes joined the boycott, and then the entire institute was involved. R. Brown called a mass rally in the theatre and asked the other presidents, Klopstock and Dr. Cunningham, to be present.

The auditorium was packed, the students excited that Van Horne finally seemed to be joining in the national sea of student unrest. At other institutions, students burned buildings and destroyed presidential offices. Van Horne had missed most of the fun, but now the students felt that this was a chance to join in, to show they were coming of age.

R. Brown addressed the rally. "I am proud to be associated with a group that is meeting to defend the rights of two fellow students from the Third World." He pointed to Winston and Benjamin so the cameras could identify them. "The regulations of this institute are oppressive and discriminatory." Brown looked at Cunningham, who looked at the ceiling. "We have tried to settle this matter sensibly, but apparently nothing can be done. They say their hands are tied. The dean's, the president's, everybody's hands are tied by the red tape of regulation. I am going to suggest soon that we go to the source, the only place that has the power to untie these hands. But let's hear from them first. The voice of the faculty."

Klopstock stood up, the bunch of tools jingling at his waist. "Look guys, don't blame us, eh? Our guys in Phys. Ed. do what they're told. They have to. So do I. But we're on your side. In your fight for individual rights, I mean. We were all students once." He glanced at his image in the TV monitor. "We're a community here, right? A community of people who have to pull together. So good luck, Winston, and er, Ben."

Dr. Cunningham stood up. "I want you all to go back to your classrooms and leave this to me. I will arrange a meeting with the Ministry next month and see if something can't be done. Put up a temporary shower stall, something like that. I am heartened by the way the students of Van Horne have rallied to their colleagues' side in their hour of distress. Off you go now."

R. Brown returned to the microphone. "Do you hear that?" he screamed. "They are powerless puppets, pawns of the government. They make a virture of impotence. Leave it to him, eh?" he continued, pointing to Cunningham. "To Big Daddy? Does that satisfy us? Did we call this meeting to be patted on the head? These people are impotent. So is the faculty. But we aren't, are we?"

The word "impotent" echoed round the hall, and the crowd roared back, outraged. "NO," they thundered, and then began chanting, "NO, NO, NO, NO," in the rhythm of potency until Brown held up his hand, and there was a burst of applause by way of climax.

"Let us show them," Brown shouted. "Let us leave now and march on the Buildings." He jumped off the stage and strode down the aisle, accompanied by his executive and Winston and Benjamin, leading the crowd into the street. Hastily-made signs appeared, vaguely inscribed because not everyone fully understood the cause. "Down with Impotence," one said. "Up with Van Horne," said another. Six hundred students formed a loose column with R. Brown at the head, and began the mile walk to the Buildings.

Alone on the dais with Klopstock, Cunningham said, "Now it's up to the minister. We've done our part."

At the Buildings, the students swarmed in front of the steps, shouting. "We want Tupper," they shouted. "We want Tupper. We want Tupper."

Inside, the minister, Percy, and Clem Stokes watched from a window.

"Press here yet?" the minister asked.

"Not yet. We sent them up to Van Horne first to catch the meeting. They'll be here shortly."

"TV?"

"On their way."

Clem Stokes said, "The kid in front with the glasses who looks like a granny is R. Brown."

"What does the 'R.' stand for?"

"Nobody knows."

"They are calling for you again, sir. We're nearly ready. Does R. Brown know you, Clem? You go out first and warm them up, then, and then bring on the minister."

Stokes stepped through the huge double doors to a roar of approval and a burst of cheering as some of his old students recognized him. Stokes waved at them, smiling, while they cheered and whistled. R. Brown raised his arms above his head. "We want Tupper," he said, and the crowd took it up again.

Between chants, Stokes said, "Why?"

The crowd stopped chanting and looked at R. Brown.

"Because he is suppressing the rights of one of our colleagues," R. Brown cried.

"Ah, come on, Brownie," Stokes said conversationally. "The minister isn't suppressing anybody except me."

"We demand the right to speak to the minister."

"You'll have to shout a bit louder than that," Stokes said, so off-handedly that only R. Brown caught it. "The minister is in conference," he said, more loudly.

R. Brown waved the crowd to begin again. "We want Tupper," they chanted.

Stokes slipped back into the Buildings. "TV's here," he said. "We're all set."

"Right," the minister said. "Let's see. I respect their sense of human justice, but laws must be observed. Then the Junius bullshit, right? Give solemn promise matter will be looked at."

"You've got it," the deputy said and pushed him firmly through the door.

When the cameras had him in focus, the minister raised his hands for quiet. Then he spoke. He spoke clearly and well on government, education, and Van Horne, then came to the present case and asked them to trust him. The crowd looked at R. Brown for guidance, ready to sack the Buildings if he gave the word. R. Brown shook hands with the minister and said, "We put ourselves in your hands," and led a round of clapping. The minister waved and disappeared. The students formed up and marched back, trying to find a song to march to, settling finally on various lyrics to the tune of "John Brown's Body."

That evening, watching the report on television, the president said to his wife, "R. Brown has an intellectual air. Looks well on TV."

"You talked too much, Gravely."

"Nobody listens, my dear. All the TV people really wanted was a quote and a shot of me picking my nose, which I don't think they got."

Up at the Buildings, one more piece of groundwork was necessary. The deputy minister phoned the leader of the opposition and persuaded him to ask a question in the legislature the next day. In exchange, the deputy minister arranged for two members of the opposition to go on a study tour, an examination of the social effects of legalizing pornography in Stockholm, Oslo, and Copenhagen.

When the question came, the minister replied that he was glad his colleague on the opposite side of the House had raised the matter and was happy to agree that such a demonstration would not have been necessary had Van Horne had the power to govern its own affairs. The problem was that even trivial questions were still referred to the Ministry, but this would now have to change. Plans were already in preparation to give Van Horne the same kind of freedom to develop as other institutions. He would have an announcement to make soon.

vi. Cockayne's Syndrome

R. BROWN CALLED IN on William from time to time. He still affected to see the future more clearly than William. "When I leave Van Horne," he said one day, "I shall be able to repair automobile steering assemblies. I may even have a degree with a major in rack-and-pinion joints, if the institute continues as it's going. You, on the other hand, will be hanging on by your fingernails unless you stay in administration."

"But will steering assemblies satisfy you?"

"We can't all be creative, sir. Or rather, we can, but not for money. Of course steering assemblies won't satisfy me. I won't hate them, though. My uncle, on the other hand, wrote editorials for a national newspaper; he was forced to sound convincing once a day for thirty years. Towards the end he said he felt like a profundity machine. You put the results of a Newfoundland by-election in one end of the machine, and thirty minutes later profundity comes out of the other. By the time he realized what he had done to himself, it was too late. In the end, he wouldn't allow a newspaper in the house."

"You don't think that will happen to you?"

"You can't be corrupted by steering assemblies. I shall fix one a day for a big fee and spend the rest of the time how I like."

"Quite the new man, aren't you."

"Yes, I am."

"What's going on?" Jane asked. "Questions in the legislature. What's up?" They were drinking cocoa and watching the news.

"I'll tell you in strictest confidence. We're going independent." He explained the implications, as he understood them.

"A board of governors? Well, well. Any idea who will be on it?"

"What does it matter? A bunch of dummies that will let Cunningham do as he likes, Gravely says. It's all image."

"Still, it would be interesting to find out, wouldn't it? Let me know if you hear. Now, put your cocoa down. I want to show you something I read about last night . . ."

Van Horne and the television were forgotten.

Mordecai came by. He was now back in his first costume of blazer, grey flannels, and a tie.

"Getting much?" William asked, doggily, picking up on their last conversation.

"Nookie, you mean?" Mordecai smiled politely but without interest. "I suppose about average. I don't think about it a lot any more. Truth is, I tend to fall asleep in front of the TV, which irritates the gals a bit. My big night, my *only* night, is Saturday, unless we go to a party. Then it has to wait until Sunday morning, and not even then if I'm hung over. You'll see."

"What are you saying? I *will* see. You've passed me? Last month you were still catching up."

"Sorry. I thought I'd told you the latest findings of my shrink. He is certain now that I am the first case of a psychological form of Cockayne's Syndrome."

¹/₂/

"What on earth is that?"

"A rare disease which ages you very rapidly, a lifetime in a couple of years or less. With me the disease is psychological, and the aging is sexual, but otherwise I have all the symptoms."

"Let me understand this. You were born two years ago? Sexually, that is. So how old are you now?"

"About thirty-five. Past the first flush. Settled down."

"Who with? May I ask?"

"I'm back with Maisie, my first love. It suits me, except that she makes me bathe more than I used to."

"Is the progress likely to continue? Or have you arrived at maturity?"

"That we don't know. Because it's psychological, it may cure itself. Perhaps this is nature's way of getting me to grow up, and I may rest here now, a decade behind my age. That would suit Maisie."

"I think it would suit a lot of people."

"That's what the shrink says. I think he's jealous. He's certainly obsessed with sex."

Left alone, William brooded over his own situation. Lately he had begun to feel less satisfied with his relationship with Jane. He had never felt himself deeply in love with her, or in love with her at all; but he had taken enormous pleasure, not just in their love-making, but in his amazing luck at having chosen, and been chosen by, someone who took such an uncomplicated view of human relationships. Lately, though, it was not enough. He confided his problem, without naming names, to Geoffrey Spindle.

Spindle said, "I have no experience to share with you, I'm afraid. I feel like a headmistress being asked to advise a schoolboy. I should have thought you had a very enviable arrangement, like something in a nineteenth-century French novel. Once a week your needs are taken care of with civility and taste, and at no cost to you. But you repine."

"It's all so perfect. Even married people are not so accommodated as I am, according to Jack Bodger. I'm bored."

"What about the Dean of Consumer Studies? Is she bored too?"

"How did you know? I've never told you."

"It wasn't especially clever. As Sherlock Holmes said, eliminate the impossible, and the improbable must be true. I've eliminated everybody else."

"You think anyone else knows?"

"Not if I'm your only confidant. Cheer up. I know what a rotten life you lead. As I say, once a week you share the bed of the handsomest woman in the institute, and the rest of the time you earn twice as much as I do for half as much work. It just goes to show, you can't live by bread alone."

It was true. What William had been too shy to tell Geoffrey was that lately his dreams had been invaded by the fair face of Gloria. One memory especially predominated, a time when he was on the back of a bus as it pulled up to a stop near the university. It was raining, and Gloria was waiting at the curb, her face wet and her hair blown across her cheek. They had not corresponded now for more than a year and he wondered if she was gone for good. He decided to try a letter.

In the House the minister rose to thank his honourable friend for returning to the point. He was ready now to announce the plan. First he outlined the history of Van Horne and gave due credit to his honourable friend for being a part of the government that had brought it into being. The time had now come, he said, to put the institute on a footing that would serve as a model for the creation of a large number of similar institutes, not yet, but at some time in the future. In the meantime he planned to give Van Horne a charter and its freedom from bureaucratic restraint by appointing a board of governors. There was some applause from all parts of the House.

vii. Homecoming

"**I** WANT YOU to meet our new Director of Community Relations, Ned Shunter. Ned is going to put us on the map. The board hired him directly."

"Public Relations?" William asked.

"It'll be my job to generate positive signals between Van Horne and its community, Bill." Shunter's curls almost touched his collar. He was wearing a blue velvet suit and a white ruffled shirt, flecked with blood where he had shaved badly. He looked like King Charles I.

"Who is the community?"

"I'm going to start with the alumni. I understand you don't have too many, so we'll have to maximize what there is. Find out where the money is. Nice meeting with you, Bill. Keep the old ivy growing. I'll do the rest." He nodded to dismiss William and turned to the president.

Two days later they met again. "We're going to have a Homecoming, William," Cunningham said. His eyes sparkled. "What a pity we don't play football."

"Some of them play hockey, I think," William said.

Shunter said, "That'll do. Leave it to me. I'll come back to you in . . ." — he looked at his watch — "two days. By the way, is there someone around here who speaks Latin?"

"Geoffrey Spindle."

"Good. I'll have him check the copy. I understand you can spell 'alumni' a couple of ways. We don't want our rivals making fun of us, do we?"

Three days later the president announced the first Annual Homecoming to celebrate the anniversary of the institute's founding.

There was a lot of work to be done. First a route had to be chosen for the Annual Homecoming Parade. The city agreed to close off two small streets for the day, and the police undertook to clear the area of drunks during the parade. Shunter was given a temporary staff to take care of publicity. Posters appeared in the subway. "Come Home to Van Horne," they said. Every student who had ever entered the doors of the institute — graduates, drop-outs, extension students — received an invitation, and a very high percentage were pleased to come.

The new board of governors became involved. They were a small group. Only six, including the deputy minister, had been appointed so far, and two of them had left immediately for a tour of the educational facilities of Australia and New Zealand. The chairman, Wesley Basingstoke, was a nearly retired owner of a drycleaning chain, and the manager of the minister's personal trust fund. The others still in town were Jim Corelli, a real estate broker, and Al "The Crusher" Klyst, a former wrestler, now a successful sports promoter.

At their first meeting, Wesley Basingstoke said, "This wingding got the minister's okay, Percy?"

"Absolutely, Wes. That's why he appointed the board, to bring the institute into the future."

"Good. Keep us in touch with what he wants, won't you."

"If he has any strong feelings, I'll let you know. I don't think we need bother him with detail."

"In the meantime, we give the president all the help he wants, eh? Let Cunningham in, then."

The deputy minister went to fetch him. "Ah, there you are, Gravely. We're a bit ahead of you. Come in and we can start. Just waiting for you, we were."

Cunningham took his place at the head of the table, and Basingstoke spoke. "Now then, Gravely. This is an inaugural meeting and I don't think we want to interfere with you yet. How are we going to conduct ourselves? I'll tell you what. You and Percy draw up a few rules for us, procedures, and we'll meet once a month." He looked around the table. Kryst and Corelli nodded their agreement. "Just tell us about this carnival before we go, will you?"

Cunningham went to the door and returned with Shunter, and turned the meeting over to him. Shunter outlined the plans for the Homecoming, answered some questions, and withdrew.

Klyst, who had been appointed to the board only the day before, said, "My old man always told me when I gave up wrestling that I'd never make it in business unless I wore a tie. I don't like being represented by some hairy son-of-a-bitch in a frilly blouse. Especially at an educational institution. Where'd you find him, Gravely?"

"*I* found him," the deputy minister said. "A lot of creative people look like that, Al. And he makes a potful, I was told."

Klyst grunted, unsatisfied, but the board formally approved the plans and adjourned to the lunch provided on a side table. Over the sandwiches, the president attempted to explain Van Horne to Klyst. The new governor softened a little after his second rye-and-ginger. He said, "Reminds me of when I started out promoting. Bareknuckle, then. Two scrubbers in a roped-off space in a barn, no limits, fifty dollars to the one left on his feet, dollar a head to get in. They've stopped it finally, but I got in at the last. Now look at me. I'm thinking of building a new stadium next year." He rolled his three hundred pounds contentedly in his chair.

"The board will be a great help to me," Cunningham said.

"'Course it will. We've all made a bundle. We know how it's done."

All through February and the first half of March they worked. Shunter appeared and disappeared, usually by taxi, several times a day.

Everyone was busy. A main feature of the Homecoming was to be a tour of the institute, including displays of each department's work. Everyone was required to participate. Departments that seemed to be dragging their feet were shouted at by a maniacally excited president. As the day approached, the control centre of the institute shifted from the president's office to the staff dining room, where Shunter had set up his headquarters.

Not every faculty member objected to eating in the students' cafeteria. "The food," Geoffrey Spindle said, "is identically nasty, but at least the students don't talk about mortgages and wine-making. And they may not be learned, but they are aware of their ignorance. On the other hand, last week one of my colleagues in the Performing Arts department asked me if I still taught 'all that bullshit about Gendrons.' It took me a while to realize he meant 'gerunds,' but when I pointed out to him that he was confusing a part of speech with the name of a baby-carriage manufacturer, he seemed completely unashamed."

Shunter's new headquarters looked like those of a well-funded candidate for election. He had now about twenty people working for him directly; indirectly the whole institute was at his disposal. The bills piled up and were ignored, except for Shunter's own expenses, which went to the deputy minister for payment. Cunningham signed all the other bills, assured that in some way they would cover their costs in the end.

William had nothing at all to do. Except within those classrooms that were not being used for displays on Homecoming day, the real work of the institute had come to a halt. He decided to close his office for the week before Homecoming and assist the president, who welcomed someone to talk to. Cunningham had decided to make his own office part of the tour. He had a gown made in brown and gold silk, which made Spindle's mouth water for the remnants it must have generated, and a squashed-in pastry-cook's hat in the same colours in velvet. The effect was vaguely medieval, "like a Doctor of Law from the University of Ulan Bator," R. Brown said. In this costume, the president planned to sit at his desk and shake hands with whoever came by.

viii. Klyst's Triumph

A T DAWN ON Saturday the police made a sweep of the surrounding streets, bundling the derelicts into vans, and transporting them to distant parks, where they wandered, lost, like animals in an unfamiliar habitat.

The first visitors were the parents from the northern part of the province, some a day's journey away, who were making a weekend of it in the city, in most cases arriving the night before to stay with married children. By nine o'clock some of them had been awake for hours and were walking the streets, waiting for something to happen. By ten o'clock, the parents who lived in the city appeared, and by noon the grounds of the institute were full.

First came the parade. Shunter had done well. Six floats represented classes that had so far graduated; three of the governors had donated a float each, complete with drivers and a few employees of the companies they owned in case there weren't enough students to cover the float; the other three floats were rented by the institute. The parade was led by a sound truck, and a clown dressed in the institute's colours was hired to bring up the rear.

William was deputed to take the board of governors on a tour. Eight of them had now been appointed and five attended

Homecoming. They met in the president's office for whisky, and after two drinks, Al Klyst said to William, "Right, Herbert, let's get it over with."

They set off for the Drug Mart and the technology displays. The Electrical department had dressed some students in clean coveralls and had mounted a little model of Niagara Falls. As the water passed over the falls and through a tiny power house it drove a generator, which lit up the display. It reminded William of a Christmas present he had been given when he was seven or eight, a kit from which a clever child could construct a watermill of waxed cardboard that worked quite realistically until the cardboard became sodden. "Cute," said Klyst.

The Welding department was less ingenious. It had posed a student with an oxy-acetylene torch solemnly cutting pieces of metal into smaller pieces. When the group reached the display, the room was already a foot deep in scraps. The group silently watched him cut a square inch of metal into two, and moved on.

The Automobile Repair department had a surprise for them. A superb yellow roadster from the twenties, immaculately restored, revolved slowly on a pedestal. At the wheel, dressed in dust-cover, cap, goggles, and gauntlets, was a papier-mâché toad. As they entered the room, the creature waved and spoke.

"Poop-poop," he called.

The governors looked at William for an explanation.

"I think it must be Toad of Toad Hall," he said.

"Poop-poop," the creature agreed.

Klyst was annoyed. "I don't know about Toad of Toad Hall," he said, "but why is this asshole dressed up like a goddam bullfrog?"

"It's a gag, Al," Basingstoke said. "Isn't it?" he asked William.

"It's a horse's ass, that's what it is," Klyst snarled.

"Poop-poop," R. Brown called from behind his goggles.

From the Drug Mart they went to the Old Folks' Home. Here they saw a cake being baked, and a nightdress being modelled. "It's Mary Jane," one of the governors said, as the minister's daughter caught his eye. "Very fine display this, Moodie."

"Real pretty," Klyst said. "Say hullo to your dad for me." He pointed to himself. "Al Klyst."

Eventually they came to the Communication Arts display in the Bible College. The Department of Related Studies had not wanted to co-operate, and William had ordered the English faculty to do something just before they backed out, too. He was curious to see what they had come up with, and he chivvied the now bored governors into the room where the display was mounted. It was nothing much. A chair had been placed on a dais. On it, Mordecai sat reading, surrounded by thirty or forty casually opened books. Above his head hung a sign, "A Good Book Is the Precious Life-Blood of a Master Spirit." The display was supposed to be viewed through a large cardboard frame which dangled by a string from the ceiling, but the distances were wrong and the frame got in the way of seeing Mordecai clearly.

"That's the master spirit, is it?" Basingstoke said.

William took a good look at Mordecai. He was wearing skin-tight jeans cut so low that some pubic hair showed. A T-shirt of cloth-of-gold that left his stomach bare was decorated with a heavy lapis lazuli necklace. In one ear he wore a set of car-keys. His feet were encased in black varnished clogs.

He smiled at William. "I found out I'm dying," he said. "Everybody is, but they don't know it. It's *the* turn-on, man. I'll come and tell you about it. There's still time for you. Stay away from those vultures." He waved at the governors.

"What's he talking about?" Klyst wanted to know. The others had moved on. "If he's dying, why's he so happy? He *is* happy, isn't he?"

"I think he's speaking cosmically, sir."

"Is he a faggot?"

"No."

"I thought this place catered to the practical side," Klyst pursued.

"We like to take care of the complete man," William said.

"Yeah? You'd better not be having me on, buddy."

There was free beer and hot dogs in the gym, and before the next stage William had time to slip away and find out what was happening to Mordecai. He found him at home, drying his hair, dressed in the same jeans but now in a kind of bead jacket like a gypsy. "You're surprised, I know, William," he said, holding a hand up before William could speak. "But I wasn't cured, after all, just moving through my conservative period. Now I know what it's all about."

"What?"

"Life, man. I'm now forty-two years old. You are still a kid. You think you're immortal but, man, I know I'm dying, and I want to grab it while I can. The kids are coming up with the answers and I'm joining them."

"But, Mordecai, you *are* forty-two. You're going bald."

"Right, but I know stuff no one else knows. I was just twenty-two and thirty-two and I remember. My shrink says that I am now going through a typical mid-life crisis. It's the time when men leave their wives, William, and the secret sailors cash their savings and head for the open seas. I'm like them. This is it, my last chance to live."

"Are you leaving your wife, too?"

"In a manner of speaking."

"Poor Maisie."

"I wasn't made for the middle-aged suburban bit. She'll find someone else. I'll wear a wig if I have to."

"So who are you — what's the word — balling?"

"The most beautiful chick in the world. We have this terrific relationship which I could never have with a middle-class white person who intellectualizes everything."

"Are you telling me you are dating a young, black illiterate girl?"

"Javanese." Mordecai put on some rings. "Tonight we hit the disco scene."

"What do you talk about?"

"Talk? Oh, Christ, William! You are about a hundred years old, you know that?"

"But what if this is just another stage? What next?"

"It's obvious, isn't it? If it's temporary, then I'm going to grab every minute. 'Bye, now."

William moved on to Beaver Palace, the national home of hockey, ice carnivals, and circuses. Here the first Annual Homecoming game was to be held between the Van Horne Broncos and the famous Greys, the Simcoe University team. The presence of the Greys had been arranged by the newest member of the board, "Bone" Bishop, a former leading amateur hockey player himself, now one of several vice presidents at Simcoe University, appointed to Van Horne's board to keep an eye on the institute on behalf of the Council of Presidents. Today Bishop saw himself in relation to Van Horne as the squire, beginning a tradition in the style of the town-and-gown or village-and-hall matches he had played in during his year at Oxford.

Beaver Palace was designed to hold thirty thousand people, and the five or six hundred Van Horne graduates, wives, and friends could not do much more than line the rail. They did this enthusiastically, however, and Klyst ordered music at full volume just as if it were Saturday night.

The Greys skated out first. They had won every trophy in the college league and were unbeaten for two seasons. Among them were four future doctors, two orthodontists, two lawyers, and several scientists. The Simcoe coaches did not have to rely on Physical Education majors like other universities: the Greys were the aristocrats of college hockey.

"I've told our men to take it easy on your lads," Bone Bishop said. "They are going to treat it as an exhibition game."

"We'll do our best," Klyst said.

When the Van Horne Broncos came out there was a ragged cheer, and then a buzz ran through the crowd, which grew until it reached the party in the governors' box. Through the hum came the mutter of names being repeated, familiar names, which echoed along the rail and turned into a single shout of joy. At the other end of the rink, the Greys stopped skating in elegant circles and stared down the ice.

"What's going on, Al?" Bishop asked Klyst, who was smiling and waving at the Broncos.

"I think they've recognized my boys," Klyst said. "Hey there, Bomber!" he waved at a scarred defenceman.

"*Your* boys. We're all involved."

One of the other governors whispered in Bishop's ear. Bone turned pale. "But that's not fair," he protested. "Cunningham, did you know about this? The Broncos are the Beavers!" he squealed, naming one of the leading professional hockey teams in Canada, the permanent residents of Beaver Palace. "We must call it off. The Greys can't play against these . . . professionals." Words had almost failed him.

"Don't be hasty, Bone," Klyst said comfortably. "It's just an exhibition. The Greys would have made Van Horne look silly. Now it'll be the other way round."

"I would never have arranged it if I'd known."

"I believe you. We're here now, though."

But Bishop would not give in. "Surely you can't claim these players as students?"

"They are, though," Klyst said. "Night students, most of them. Very enterprising man, the Dean of Extension."

Before Bishop could reply, the referee called the teams to centre ice and dropped the puck. Ivan "The Goon" Koretski, the Beaver policeman, waited only until the Greys' wing man had the puck, then skated over and broke his nose. The Greys swarmed around, fists raised, but were flicked away by the Bronco-Beavers. The Goon was assessed two minutes for high-sticking. From the face-off, the Bronco-Beavers collected the puck and gave it to each other for a few moments, then scored. Then they did it again. The centre for the Greys, an intern in psychiatry, lost his temper and tried to hit one of the Beavers. The Beaver reached forward, pulled the arms of the psychiatrist's sweater down, tied them in a knot, then hit him a dozen times around the ears.

The crowd was delighted; this was as good as the games on television. But it clearly could not continue. After four more goals, Klyst walked reluctantly to the Beaver-Bronco bench and spoke to the coach. "Be all right, now, Bone," he said when he returned.

Now the Beavers played flawless, positional hockey, allowing the Greys to foul as they pleased, brushing them off without retaliation. When they had established a lead of twelve goals, the coach sent out one or two genuine Van Horne students, who had been dressed for show. For the rest of the game, the Beaver-Broncos fed the Van Horne students passes that gave them easy shots on goal, sometimes avoiding the empty net themselves to reassemble and return with a student in place. They ignored their opponents, except to take the puck off them after a face-off, and towards the end of the game two misjudgements allowed the Greys to score. The final score was Van Horne 22, Simcoe 2.

Klyst was the hero. He reacted modestly. "You pay for the best and that's what you get. I've got the best."

ix. Cunningham's Dream

AFTER THE HOCKEY came the banquet, held at Mendosa's
Folly, a celebrated landmark, a monstrosity of red sand-
stone built in the form of a castle by the son of an immigrant
who had made a fortune in the goldfields, and then abandoned
when he went bankrupt.

Two hundred came to the banquet, which went through its
usual Canadian course of courses: shrimps in ketchup, chicken
and peas, ice cream and coffee. There were wine glasses, and
one bottle of wine for every six diners. At the end, the president tink-tink-tinked on his glass and the room fell silent.

Dr. Cunningham rose. It was his night and he spoke well
and at length. He discussed the etymolgy of "technology,"
finding in its Greek root unlimited scope for Van Horne's
future. He moved on to educational institutes in general, possible models for Van Horne, and inevitably referred to Plato's
Academy, the book of nature, the lessons of life, and the joke
Mark Twain made about his father's ignorance. He came back
then to Van Horne, its beginnings, and its struggles to find a
place in the sun. He was never boring; he avoided the subject
of young people today; he made no appeal for funds; and most
of all he made no attempt at humour. He was inspired, and
spoke for thirty minutes, keeping silent such different audi-
ences as Al Klyst, R. Brown, and Bone Bishop. His vision
captured him, and they all waited for the revelation.

"And so tonight," he said, returning to earth, "tonight we come to celebrate the anniversary of dear old Van Horne." He smiled for the first time to show he was now speaking lightly. "It is the first of these occasions, the first of many we hope, but in one way I hope it will be one of the last." There was a silence. "Not that we shan't survive; rather, I live with the hope that in another ten years we shall look back on this occasion with affection and wonder, when the president of Van Horne Technical *University* will remember the institute's origins as he offers the toast I offer you now. To the future."

They were moved and excited. Some of the governors were disturbed. They knew the power of the public announcement, how difficult it was to unsay it, and they had understood that one of their functions was in just this area, to keep a lid on Cunningham until the minister had decided what he wanted to do with Van Horne.

Klyst jumped in right away. "Very nice speech, Gravely. All bullshit, of course. This isn't a university, never will be. I know what a university is. My boy goes to one. This isn't one. Still, does no harm to dream a bit."

But Cunningham couldn't hear. Dazed by his own words, he sat smiling at everyone through a pink mist.

After the dinner they danced. R. Brown had brought a very beautiful girl a head taller than himself, and William led off by asking her to dance, while his own date, Maisie, was talking to Klyst. William rather thought he might cut Brown out, having the advantage, he felt, in height, age, looks, and general suitability. When the first set was over, they returned to the table and R. Brown called out cheerily, "You are wasting your time with that one, sir. She only likes small men with horn-rimmed glasses, don't you, Doris?" For the rest of the evening she refused to dance with anyone except Brown.

At one o'clock the bar closed, the lights went up, and the band played "The March of the Gladiators." There were shouts of "Make way!" and the sounds of dogs barking, and then into the ballroom swept a long wheeled sled drawn by a dog team whipped up by Al Klyst, shouting "Mush!" On the sled, which was forty feet long, was the buffet supper. When they realized what it was, the crowd broke and ran, and there was a difficult moment when it looked as if the sled would be overturned, especially the centrepiece, which consisted of a huge pile of lobsters. But half a dozen graduates of journalism quickly formed a chain and took the lot. Order was restored, mostly by Klyst, and many of the lobsters returned, and the crowd formed up to get the rest of the food. Klyst stood proudly to one side, holding his whip. "I thought of this myself," he said.

And then it was time to go. The governors left first, and finally only Cunningham, William, and R. Brown, and their ladies, were left at the head table. William felt he ought to stay near the president, who was still drunk with his vision, smiling and bobbing his head at everyone who came by. When he was finally got into a taxi, R. Brown offered William and Maisie a lift home or "wherever." "There are after-hours boîtes," he said. "Even in this town."

But it was time to go.

An hour later William had told Jane about the evening. "I have no idea what is going on," he said. "I don't understand anything about anything." He had managed to get more than his share of wine, and he was undressing slowly, reflectively. "Light years ago, when I first came to Van Horne, one of the students called me a dodo."

"R. Brown."

"Yes. You know in all the ways that you can divide up people, one way is to divide them into those who know what is going on and those who don't. It has nothing to do with intelligence. It's a separate faculty essential for politicians, I would think. I have the feeling that I don't know what is going on most of the time these days, with the board, with the students — especially with R. Brown — even with the president. Though I think the president is as out of it as I am most of the time, except when he's with me. I even have the feeling you know what's going on, always have, always will. And I don't."

"Does anyone know everything that's going on?"

"Geoffrey Spindle does."

"You know that, then."

"Yes, that's something, isn't it?"

"Did you *ever* know?"

"In graduate school, and at Cambridge. I knew there, all right. That's my point, I think. I think one should always stay where one knows what's going on." He fell back gently on to the bed, one foot still entangled in his trousers.

"You are getting too Eng. Lit. mystical for me. But by the look of this, something ought to be going on right now."

"There you are, you see. That was between you and it. I didn't know that was going on. Can you believe it? This must be what it's like for Mordecai. Was, I should say."

"Now that you both know, let's start from there."

Afterwards, over a cup of tea before he left, she said, "Tell me about the other governors. What was their reaction to the speech?"

And for another half-hour William recounted the events of the evening. Then, as always, because it seemed courteous, he suggested that he stay, but this time he was more relieved than cast down when, as always, she sent him on his way.

x. The Robes of Office

THE NEXT MEETING of the board of governors was held without the president. The meeting had been called by Wesley Basingstoke at the deputy minister's suggestion. It took place on Klyst's estate, a thousand-acre farm fifty miles from the city. Here, around the barbecue pit, the board and the deputy minister gathered.

"Sixty, eh? I shouldn't have thought that was too old, especially in education," Lytton Gormley, an octogenarian, said.

"These kids want someone they can relate to," Basingstoke said.

"Why? Are we running an orphanage?"

"Someone closer to their concerns," Corelli explained.

Gormley looked unenlightened, then bored. They had been talking about it for half an hour and he was tired. "It doesn't matter, anyway. The minister wants to get rid of him. That right, Wes?"

Basingstoke nodded. "We just have to work out the form," he said.

"What's to work out?" Klyst wondered. "Call him in, buy his contract, and tell him to fuck off."

"This isn't a hockey goalie, Al. In the educational game they sometimes get a year's notice."

"So what do we do?"

Basingstoke ticked off his fingers. "In two weeks we'll tell Cunningham. I'll get him up here for the day. We'll let his successor know the day before, so that he's ready to move in. We'll find Gravely something else. Any ideas, Bone?"

"I've taken care of that."

"Right. So we make up a nice package and announce that the whole thing is done for Cunningham's benefit at his request."

Klyst said, "As I said, buy out his contract, and tell him to fuck off."

"Who takes over, Wes?"

"The minister says we should put in a temporary for the time being. The obvious one is Moodie."

"Why should Gravely take it lying down?"

"We'll make it worth his while. If he doesn't make a fuss, Bone, here, will fix him up with an honorary Doctor of Laws at Simcoe. He'll like that."

"What do you have in mind for him, Bone?"

"Supervisor of Education for the Prison System. A man who used to teach here suggested it. He runs one of the training schools."

"Dunvegan?"

"That's the man."

"He still won't like it."

Nor did he.

"I suppose it's no good my appealing to the minister?"

"None at all, Gravely. He's been consulted."

"What happens if I go to the papers. Kick up a stink?"

"No degree. And we would have to reveal the cost of the Homecoming."

"Shunter did all that. I don't know anything about it."

"You signed the bills. Shunter's personal bills were minuscule, so the deputy minister says. Yours look pretty big."

"Who will take over?"

Basingstoke looked at the slip of paper in his hand. "You'll have to ask the minister that."

"Is he behind my desk now?"

"Oh, no. You have to announce it first. When you're ready."

"What do I say?"

"All the usual bumf, something about not standing on the order of your going, Percy suggested."

"It sounds as though I could be gone tomorrow night."

"A rest might be a good idea. After a breakdown like you've had. Two weeks in the sun. Our expense, of course."

"No thanks. I think I'll watch the last act."

"Just as you like. But you will tell the papers, won't you? Tomorrow."

"I'll tell them."

Convocation was held the week after Gravely Cunningham had been invested with the robes of Doctor of Law at Simcoe University. Thus, for the Van Horne ceremony, he had the choice of two sets of robes. He led the academic procession in the glorious brown and gold silks of the presidency of Van Horne, and he wore this robe for his farewell speech, which was graceful and becoming. When he had finished speaking, he slowly took off his robe, laid it on the podium and donned his other, doctoral, gown. ("I thought for a minute he was going to flash us," Klyst said, later.)

Basingstoke gathered his wits first, and leaped to his feet to lead the applause as the president strode off the stage.

xi. Tupper for Premier

THE CONVENTION WAS nearing its climax. The candidates for party leader, and therefore premier, had been narrowed down to five. Of these, four could be considered serious. The fourth and weakest was the Minister of Rural Affairs, Mervin Watkins, a man from the traditional heartland of the party whose support, though insufficient to get him elected, was faithful and his to send where he would. So far, Watkins had insisted he was in to win, but he would certainly be eliminated after the next vote and soon he would send his supporters in the direction of his choice.

The third man was a sporting lawyer with liberal sympathies who was thought to be the choice of the young Turks. He led on the first ballot, but his support had shrunk steadily with each succeeding vote. If he could garner Watkins's supporters, though, he might last another round.

Most people saw the race as between the candidates who were first and second at this stage. The leader was a solid businessman, part-owner of several mines, a sleeping partner in a large, old law firm. His sole drawback was that he had never run for office, never contested an election. His experience of politics was deep, but all of it had happened offstage. There were plenty of safe seats available if he should win, but some delegates, who had failed themselves to get a nomination after years of trying, found him offensive in his role of the rich amateur come from the world of business to show these politicos how to run their affairs. He had spent a fortune on the convention, and for that he was clinging to a narrow lead.

The minister was second. He had begun as low as fifth while his ultimate supporters voted sentimentally in the early unimportant voting. His share of the vote had steadily increased with every ballot.

New results were announced, and now the fifth candidate, in the race only to test whether the times would yet allow a Chinese, freed his supporters to do as they liked.

Now the serious search began. Recruiters from the top two men bargained for the support of Mervin Watkins, who was now a spent force. The front runner offered him the choice of cabinet posts, and a list of patronage appointments topped up with a little package of directorships. The minister offered nothing for Watkins himself — that could be settled later, quietly. Much more important for an old man, the minister offered him a memorial, to him and to the rocks and stones and trees in his riding. He offered him a college, built in his riding, to be devoted to the study of the things that were in the interest of his constituents: fishing, logging, and the operation of tourist camps. It would be, the minister's aide said, the Van Horne of the north (already the phrase meant something), and, eventually, the Watkins Technological University.

"The Athens of the Bush," Watkins said, and smiled. The aide added one more word. "These colleges are going to make the traditional universities sit up," he said. "The minister is very keen on them."

It was brilliant and decisive. Watkins had finished high school, the last two years by correspondence, not quite by the light of an oil lamp but by the uncertain flicker of a forty-watt bulb powered by a gasoline generator in the barn. When he graduated, he had been refused entrance to Simcoe University. He had kept the grudge to himself, like a good politician, and now he would get his reward. "Tell Joe not to worry," he said to the aide. He turned to his people, slowly so that the TV cameras had time to focus. "My loyal supporters," he said. "It is time to thank you and release you from any obligation you feel to me. I am deeply grateful for your support thus far. I will not presume to direct you whom to vote for now — that is not the way this great party works. Make your choice in the knowledge that with such a fine slate of candidates you can't go wrong." The cameras disappeared, and he concluded, "Now git in there and vote for Joe."

On the next ballot the sporting lawyer fell to the bottom of the list, and after one more count Al Klyst, the floor manager, at home in his own stadium, raised the hand of the next premier.

"The summer is it, Percy? Have to manage on my own after that, will I?" The new premier played in his new chair, testing the casters by pushing himself around the huge office from the historic desk to the sheet of windows overlooking the park, to the door concealing the private shower, back to the desk again. "Whee!" he cried.

"What are you going to call me for the next three months?" the deputy minister asked.

"Anything you like, Percy baby." The premier shot over to the window. "Whee!" he cried. "How about 'Senior Deputy Minister'?"

"A bit cumbersome, and besides, when I'm gone you might have a powerful job with no one you want to give it to. You want something that dies with me."

"You think of everything, don't you?"

"Well, we *are* here."

"Yes, we made it. Whee! So have your three wishes."

"First, call me something like Senior Co-ordinator. Tell the press I have a limited assignment to streamline the office."

"All right, that's one. What else? Give me a push, would you?"

The premier climbed on to the seat of the chair and crouched there as the deputy gave a little run and launched him across the room.

"The Education ministry will need a new deputy, sir. Won't be for long, of course, but we don't want to give any hint yet, do we . . ."

"Who? Give us another push while you're talking."

"I'll know in a couple of days."

"Clem Stokes? The man you got from Van Horne?"

"No, Clem's coming back with me. I need him as vice president."

"Ah. In that case. Let me tell you first what I have in mind, and you might want to install Stokes a bit earlier, to keep your ass covered." The minister then outlined his notion of fulfilling his convention pledges for a leaner, tighter cabinet.

The deputy minister pondered this new development. "In that case, we'd better move right away."

"I don't want anything to leak out yet. I thought we'd do it in July, when the legislature's not in session, but the papers are looking for news."

"I have a personnel problem that I thought I'd taken care of. Now I'll have to move more quickly. I can manage it, I think."

"Anything else?"

"I need a holiday. This may be my last chance for a long time."

"Sure. Where shall we send you? Study tour of the south of France? Something like that?"

"No, sir. A real holiday. I'll pay for it myself."

"Why?"

"I don't think the taxpayers will want to finance my wedding trip, do you?"

The premier stayed in the corner of the room, where the chair had taken him. "Wedding, Percy? After all this time? I thought you were a confirmed bachelor. Tell the truth, I thought you were one of the boys. We all did."

"I know that. That's why I'm getting married. It doesn't matter for a senior civil servant. In fact I found it useful; but I can't have rumours like that floating around in future."

"Who is she?"

"Mrs. Hawks."

"Casey's widow? The one you bring to the picnics?"

"My girlfriend. Yes."

"But you've known her for years. We all thought she was your front."

"Now you know different."

"Well, well, well. What a crafty bastard you are! All right. But you've done the party some service. I'll get them to pay for it out of party funds. How much will the trip cost?"

"About five thousand. I'm going to treat her to the Concorde."

"And that's just about as much as they'll stand for. Right you are. Give us another push before you go."

The premier shot across the room and banged into the wall. "Whee!" he cried.

The board met after the convocation, privately, at first.

Basingstoke said. "We'll make a public announcement that the position is open. Applications will be received until June first, say. Then make the appointment for the first of

September. Percy said he'll be ready by then. He's got a man coming in as vice president to look after the shop during the summer. Have to interview one or two people, of course, including Moodie, but that's normal. In the meantime, we have to appoint Moodie acting president."

"For a month? Why?"

"I'm not sure, Al. But Percy seems to know what he's doing. There's some kind of shuffle going on. In the meantime, we have to look as if we are appointing Moodie for the foreseeable future. We don't want it to look rigged. So let's give him a warm welcome. Let's have him in."

Klyst opened the door and led William to his seat. Basingstoke began. "The important thing, Bill, is for you to represent the institute well. Gravely was a fine man, but he didn't always project the right image. A president shouldn't drive a sub-compact."

"That's right, Moodie. Look like a president, not a piker. Don't forget, it's not your money. Or ours." Klyst grinned around the table.

"Al's a joker," Basingstoke said. "Seriously, Bill, how can we help you? What about a club? Do you have one? Somewhere to take the institute's guests? Don't try and feed any of your guests in that cafeteria."

"You mean like the Upper Canada Club, or the Simcoe?"

"Well, no. Those are *my* clubs. You'd want somewhere more private. What about one of those health clubs with a restaurant? Not the Roof Top, that's mine, too. What about the one down the street here?"

"That would be very nice."

"I'll look after that," Klyst said.

"That's right, you have an interest in it, right, Al?"

"I own the sucker."

"Fine, then. And the Board of Trade club? Anyone can join that. You won't see much of us there, though we all belong. It's handy if you get caught in the rain. I think they have a golf course, don't they, Bone?"

"I believe they do, Wes, yes."

"So. Anything else, Bill?"

"What about my present job?" William asked.

"Vice president? Why don't you do what we've done? Appoint an acting one first. Then if it doesn't work out, you're not stuck with him. Especially if you should be made permanent." He consulted a note in his hand. "How about a woman? That would look well. We've heard good things about one of the deans, a Jane Goray. You know her?"

"Yes, she would be my recommendation, too."

"That's fine. Which one is she? Fair-haired girl? Glasses? Big boobs?"

"No. Dark-haired and quite thin." William restrained the impulse to add, "and little, pointed boobs."

"Put her name through, then. We'll look after it. Tell her now, if you like. Good luck, then, Bill. Anything else?"

"Yes. Can I have a holiday? Before it gets too busy?"

"Whenever you like. You've done a wonderful job as VP and we owe you. What did you have in mind? Study tour of Europe, that kind of thing?"

"Just two weeks in the fresh air."

"Little conference somewhere?"

"Just a holiday."

"On your own? A vacation, like?"

"Yes."

"Pretty hard for us to help you there, Bill."

Klyst chimed in. "No problem. I'll find him a bed at my lodge. How would that suit, Bill? Best salmon fishing in North

America. Fly in from Quebec City. I'll phone them, tell them to send a plane for you. Want to take a friend? For the night-trolling?" Klyst winked.

"I don't want to go fishing. I just want two weeks off, by myself."

"If that's what you want."

Klyst supplied the answer. "Young Bill here has got something cooking on the back burner he doesn't want us to know about." He chuckled. "A sweetie-pie. That's allowed, eh?"

Jane said, "If you don't mind a small joke, I never thought I'd be looking up to the president in quite this way."

"Shut up for a minute. I've got a lot on my mind and I'm trying to concentrate on this."

Later, she said, "It's a bit like William Pitt, isn't it? Prime minister at twenty-one? You must be the youngest president in the country."

"Acting."

"How long will that go on for?"

"The board is going to advertise the position. Mr. Basingstoke said the board is much more concerned to find the right man than rush into it. Privately he told me he thinks I have a good chance to show I'm that man."

"It sounds very good. But supposing, just supposing, they really throw it open. Do you think a woman might have a chance?"

"You mean you? Why not? Then your joke would work the other way, wouldn't it?"

"How do you mean?"

"Then I'd be looking up to you. Like this."

Klyst was wrong. Two days later, William managed to get enrolled in a tennis camp in Pennsylvania, where he spent ten days trying once more to acquire a good second serve. He returned from the vacation a day early, and only then would Klyst have guessed right.

"Do you feel like a president?" Jane asked him that night.

"I feel like a vice president, right now."

"You can have one, too, but answer my question first."

"As a matter of fact, now I feel like one of those wartime doubles they used in order to fool would-be assassins of people like Churchill. I have the feeling that at any moment the door will fly open and Wesley Basingstoke will walk in with the police. Beside him will be someone who looks like me who will be the man they meant to appoint to my job."

"There you go again, being mystical. Anyway, I don't particularly want to lay a ghost."

"That was a very bad joke. Let's talk about something else. Or better yet, let's shut up."

xii. King for a Day

WILLIAM FOUND A new world waiting for him at the president's desk. Already there were invitations to eleven different functions addressed to him personally, besides several dozen addressed to the "President." He could spend all his time attending lunches, receptions, and every possible kind of fund-raising dinner. He was invited to the Italian embassy to meet his favourite film director. On the same day he could attend the opening of a new community centre in the Portuguese quarter. The Junior Chamber of Commerce wanted him to stand for "Rising Young Man of the Month" and he was urged to jog around the slums with some show-business celebrities in a campaign to save a "people's" theatre slated for demolition.

He rang for his secretary, and while he waited, considered the two possible ways of dealing with her, as a servant or as a Jeeves. He chose the latter. "I need help, Miss Tepperman," he said, pointing to the pile of paper on his desk.

"I thought you might want to see it all just this once," she said, and swept it into a tray. "I'll sort it out."

She returned twenty minutes later with a small list she thought he ought to look at. They agreed that he would refuse all invitations for the present. They discussed the kind of coffee he liked and who should be allowed to see him without an appointment (R. Brown and Geoffrey Spindle). He turned his attention to the list she had given him, and half an hour later his day's work was done. After that it was easy. He attended to business for the first hour of the day, and spent the rest of the time reading confidential files and chatting to one or two senior administrators, chiefly Jane.

Spindle was still his best chief adviser. "There are two kinds of presidents," he said when they met on the second day of his incumbency. "The open-door kind and the closed-door kind. The closed-door kind cause less offence. If you leave your door open, people can see that you are always talking to other people they don't trust and so are too busy to see them. If your door is closed, then whoever does get in to see you feels very privileged."

So William closed his door and saw no one except at his own request. On an impulse in his first week he asked Mordecai to see him to show he hadn't forgotten his old friends in his flight to the top. Mordecai was still in beads and chains, and William was curious to know if he had settled down.

"I seem to be, old boy, but I've been getting awfully tired of late, trying not to miss anything."

There was one sad note waiting for him when he returned from Pennsylvania, but it was easily quieted. His father wrote to him, not his usual brief scrawl, but several pages, closely written.

It's not easy to write this to your own son, he began, *but I don't know where else to turn. Truth is, I'm in a bind. You remember that time you wanted to come over and I was going to Sicily with a friend? I'll cut a long story short. She turned out to be a snake. She's gone now, and I'm being sued for her debts, which are much bigger than I can manage. If I can't pay I'll lose everything. Be out on the street. I've got to raise the wind for two thousand pounds or I'm in the workhouse. I know you'll have your own obligations by now, but I write in the hope that you can spare a few bob. Anything would help. See, what happened . . .*

The letter went into the details of the deception, and ended, *The only other thing I can think of is for me to come out there, with you. I expect you could put me up in a corner. How about it?*

The ending alarmed William much more than the beginning, as it was intended to. He looked at his bank account, and on the strength of his new appointment, negotiated a small loan to top it up and sent off two thousand pounds the next day.

xiii. Free Again

THE BOARD MET on the last day of May to consider the applications, of which there were a hundred and eighty-seven, including several well-known figures in higher education, testament to Van Horne's growing reputation. Bone Bishop said of one applicant, "Well, well. I didn't know *he* was looking for a job."

Basingstoke said, "These applications are absolutely confidential, Bone."

"Of course. But he must have forgotten that I'm on the board here."

They boiled the list down to three: William, Jane Goray, and the deputy minister.

Basingstoke said, "I think I've got it now. We'll give this woman lunch to show how far *they've* got in the last few years, and then we'll do Moodie on Saturday morning. We'll announce Percy on Monday. I'll have a word with Moodie after the interview."

Klyst, who had not been fully briefed, said, "Do we have to take Percy? I kinda liked this Moodie guy."

Basingstoke said, "We are perfectly free to make up our own minds, Al, but — I wasn't going to bother you with this — there's some suspicion that Moodie has been in trouble with the police for indecent exposure. An incident in Niagara

Falls, on the American side. I got a call from a deputy chief of police, who'd been in touch with his colleagues over the border. They didn't proceed with the charges out of consideration for us, but I thought you ought to know."

"That policeman called me, too," Gormley said. "Man with a Welsh accent? I wasn't going to say anything unless Moodie looked like having a chance."

"That settles it," Klyst said. "You can't have the president waving it around. I thought that was what Cunningham was into. Remember? Convocation? Probably why Moodie turned down our help for his little holiday. He wanted a few days at a nudist camp to relieve the tension."

"I don't think that's valid psychologically, Al."

"No? Well, let's get on. The ball game's already started."

After the interview, Basingstoke and William sat together on the large couch supplied for informal metings.

"You did well in there, Bill," Basingstoke said.

"Thank you, sir."

"And the board wishes me to convey to you their appreciation of the way you've looked after things these last few weeks. You're young, Bill, and there's a great future for you somewhere."

"Thank you."

"But let me get to the point. Under the circumstances, we felt that it would be in the best interests of the institute to appoint someone with a wider experience of management than you've had."

"Not me?"

"No, Bill."

"Miss Goray?"

"Not her, either."

"Who, then?"

"The deputy minister."

"I see. Thank you very much." William stood up.

Basingstoke watched him warily. "What next, Bill?"

"Back to vice president." William was surprised at the question.

"I think the new president will be bringing in his own man, Bill. That's usual. I understand he'll be in the office on Monday."

"So I'll go back to teaching, I suppose."

"Not here, though."

"Of course. Why not?"

"You'd be an embarrassment to the new president, don't you see?"

"No, I don't. Anyway, I've got tenure."

"I have to remind you, Bill, the president is not a member of the Faculty Association. The contract doesn't apply. Didn't you negotiate it with Klopstock?"

"But I'm only acting."

"Klopstock assures me it's the same thing as far as the Faculty Association is concerned."

"So I have no rights at all?"

"The board would like to show it's gratitude. There'll be a little bonus on this month's salary. You can pick up the cheque tonight, before you leave."

"Thank you."

When Basingstoke had gone, William telephoned Jane. "We both lost, have you heard? I'll come over."

"Not now, William. I'm a bit busy. I'm moving up to the Ministry next week. They've asked me to be the new assistant deputy."

"I see. Good luck, then."

It was a shock, but not a disaster. In spite of the constant flattery of the people who depended on his goodwill, he had never believed in his career as an administrator, perfectly aware that in each promotion he had filled a vacuum, and he was not sorry now that his progress was over. But the question of what to do next loomed. Teaching, he knew, was no longer possible, or not for a while. No one would hire a former college president, even an acting one, as a junior instructor. The time had come to return to his original purpose in coming to this country, a purpose now reinforced by his stay at Van Horne.

Once more he took down the atlas from his shelves and studied the map of Canada. Having no reason to choose east over west, or near over far, he consulted Geoffrey Spindle.

"The bush?" Geoffrey asked. "In what sense?"

"In the sense of 'roughing it' as my predecessor did. In her case she roughed it near Peterborough, but that's all built over. I was wondering if there's any of it left, anywhere."

"What?"

"The bush. Not the real bush, I suppose, but, well, Canada. I like it here, but I might as well be in Wolverhampton or Buffalo. There's nothing Canadian about what has happened to me so far. I'm continually meeting people who tell me that this isn't the real Canada, that I ought to see the real Canada."

"Where is it? The real Canada?"

"It depends. Wherever these people come from, usually. A Ukrainian who teaches retailing claims that the prairies, where his grandfather cleared the land, is the real Canada. A man born on Vancouver Island claims that he comes from the real place. An engineer I had lunch with the other day claims it is up in the Arctic, because that's where he got his first job after university. Solly, who is teaching me to play squash, even claims that the real Canada is to be found in Newfoundland, because that's where *his* family started their new life when they came from India. He may have been pulling my leg, though."

"You notice that none of these people have stayed in the real Canada."

"Yes, but they know where it is. They've experienced it. I haven't."

Spindle folded over a corner and put in a tacking stitch. "As I understand it, you want to go on a sort of quest, get lost in the barrens, go over prairie trails, *etc. etc.* in search of the romantic image of Canada that has come to you from your childhood reading, reinforced by a mystical kinship you feel with your namesake, whose diaries you are now reading symbolically. She and her kind, the nineteeth-century immigrants, found themselves by losing themselves in the Canadian Shield. You want to know if this is still necessary or even possible. I don't know. It's an immigrant's question. I don't have to answer it. My great-grandfather earned me the right to find myself at home here from birth. Some of us belong hereabouts. My own great-grandfather was a successful lawyer here; the building that housed his office is now protected. But I'm digressing. Do I have you right, or am I talking a lot of balls?"

"No. I mean, no, you aren't talking a lot of balls; yes, that is what I want to know."

"Then show me that atlas." He pointed with a clean, bony finger. "There, would be my guess. There must be bits of the original there still."

"But there's hardly anything marked."

"That's the point. There are still lakes where no white man has ever set foot. Or paddled. I would think so, anyway."

So William picked a place as close to the centre as he could find, a place from which to start, and three days later he boarded the bus for the journey. The bonus promised by the board had turned out to be a month's pay, and by the time all his debts were settled and he had paid for his ticket, he was left with about three hundred dollars; enough, he felt sure, to live on until something turned up.

III
Roughing It
in the Bush

i. Loon Lake

TWO DAYS LATER, William was leaning over the rail that ran along the lakefront of a small town as close to his map destination as he could get. After thirty-six hours on the bus he had seen a sign, "Showers," outside a truck stop. The sun was shining on the lake, and he was dirty, tired, and insufficiently fed, so he climbed off the bus, stood under three dollars' worth of hot water, ate two hamburgers, and walked down to the lake.

In a little while he was going to have to find somewhere to sleep because the day, which had started out hot and blue, was cooling rapidly and turning grey. On the eastern horizon the clouds were already black. He was not concerned, because he had seen several motels with "Vacancy" signs. Tomorrow he would start looking for work.

Below him, on the town dock, two men in work shirts and yellow boots were scurrying around under the direction of a short, heavily built man with a brush cut and a cheerful expression. They were racing to load a huge pile of luggage and supplies on to a float plane, while two other middle-aged, expensively dressed men watched. As William looked on, a jeep drove on to the dock and unloaded two more expensively dressed men and another pile of luggage. Simultaneously, a gust from the approaching storm picked up a wave from the lake and flicked it over the dock. The workers stopped to look up at the sky and wipe away the drops of water, then flung themselves into the job of getting the luggage aboard before the heavy rain arrived.

It was obvious that, even with the pilot's help, they were short-handed for the task, and William trotted down the ramp to help. Fifteen minutes later the luggage was loaded, the four expensively dressed men had been stuffed aboard, and the sky cracked open. The two workers jumped into the plane and William felt a hand on his arm.

"Need a job?" the man with the brush cut asked.

William, exhilarated from having helped to cope with the emergency, heard the call and felt a readiness to heed it, a will to respond, which he knew might never come again. He had known often the readiness without the call, and he had heard the call at least once before and always regretted not respond-ing to it then, and had wondered since if he would ever hear it again, so that now, hearing it again, clear but faint, he knew he had to answer. "Yes," he said.

"Room and board and twenty a day," the man said. "Move your ass if you're coming." He ran to untie the plane from the dock as the pilot started the engine. William raced up the ramp to retrieve his bag, and two minutes later the plane tax-ied out to the middle of the lake and took off.

The noise inside the plane precluded conversation, but one of the men got close enough to William to shout in his ear.

"How're they biting?" he wanted to know, and William realized, first, that these men were already on the plane when he was hired on the dock and therefore mistook him for an old hand and, second, that they were fishermen of some kind and the plane was taking them to a place where he, William, had a job. From a variety of possible responses he chose one that he thought he could adapt to cover whatever the truth turned out to be. "Hard," he shouted back.

The man looked surprised, and conveyed the message to his companion, who passed it on to the other two fishermen, who considered in their turn what it might mean, but the noise was too great to cross-question William. Thus he began his next impersonation.

The four expensively dressed sportsmen sat on little seats that pulled down from either side of the plane. William and the other workers sat on piles of life-jackets on the floor. The only windows were the ones the pilot used in the front, so William made himself as comfortable as he could in the semi-darkness and waited. Twenty minutes later the plane bounced twice then roared across another lake. The pilot cut the engine and motioned to William to open the door. Someone caught the door from the outside and latched it back against the plane. Beyond the doorway William could see through the deluge a dozen soaking-wet men balancing on a huge square floating dock, holding on to the wing of the plane as the waves lifted it and tried to smash the plane against the dock.

"Come on, get those guys out," shouted one of the workers on the dock, to William. William gestured the men forward, and held the first one in the doorway like a parachute instructor positioning a novice for his first jump; the two workers on the dock waited until the sill of the doorway was level with the dock and lifted the man clear. One by one, they plucked the other three off the plane, and William and the two workers threw out the baggage. Finally the other workers jumped clear and William thought he had seen enough to know how to do it and jumped for the dock, missed it, and plunged into the lake. Four hands grabbed him when he surfaced and pulled him out before he could disappear under the dock.

There was no time to ponder his rescue: everyone was needed to hold the wing and keep the plane clear of the dock until the pilot started the engine and bumped across the lake to disappear into the rain-filled sky.

The sportsmen and their baggage were made to disappear, but there was no respite. William was absorbed immediately into the gang of workers on the dock as a second plane appeared and lurched over the waves towards them. Again the wing had to be caught, held clear of the dock, and the plane swung around, unloaded, and sent on its way. By now the dock was heaving so violently that it was an effort to maintain balance, but everyone was so thoroughly soaked that falling down was unimportant. The emergency continued. Supplies brought in by the two planes had to be ferried up to the kitchen and stores; a cable holding the two halves of the dock together broke and had to be replaced before the second cable went and the dock turned into a raft; a dozen small boats had to be dragged higher and higher up the shore as the waves pursued them. William lent a hand everywhere until finally the crew-cut man announced that he couldn't bring any more planes in until the storm eased, and the men ran for cover, and William stood alone beside him, watching the boiling lake.

"Sonofabitch, eh?" the man said, cheerfully. "Let's get inside."

William followed him off the dock and up along a path through the woods to an old log cabin, one of several strung along the path. "This one's empty," the man said. "Pick any bed you like. You got some dry clothes in that bag?"

William said, "Not for this."

"Just duds, eh? Find a bed. I'll be back."

He returned in a few minutes with a pair of thick khaki pants and a bush shirt. "Belonged to a guy about your size.

Died of exposure here last week." He laughed to show either that he was joking or that he found the truth funny. He looked down at William's loafers. "You want to get yourself a pair of boots," he said. "What size you take?"

"Nine."

"I'll bring you a pair from town. Take it off your pay." He pointed farther up the path. "Dining room's up there. Supper's now 'til seven; breakfast's at six, closes at six-thirty. I'll git you up at five-thirty. What's your name?"

"William Moodie."

"Yeah? Well, I'm Harry Bullock and this is my place. Take it easy, William Moodie. By the way, where did you work before?"

"I was a college president."

Bullock roared with laughter. "Jesus Christ," he said between little spurts of glee. "Now I've heard it all. College president. Jesus Christ. That's terrific. College president." And he disappeared, still laughing.

Now William sat on the bed and tried to piece together the fragmentary impressions of the last three hours, tried to assemble the tiny, vivid close-ups into a picture. He had volunteered his casual help in an emergency, much in the way he might have assisted someone to change a tire, and as a result he had passed through a door into the world that was always behind such doors, strange and wonderful. By not asking any questions, by simply doing the small needful thing that came to hand without trying to understand what it was a part of, he had been as useful in the storm as anyone, and therefore he was to be allowed to stay here. There was no way of guessing what next he would be asked to do, but the chances were fairly good that, whatever it was, he would never have done it before. He would take it a step at a time.

He slid out of the wet clothes and dried himself, then assumed the new clothes that Bullock had left him. He was cold now, and he turned to the wood stove in the middle of the cabin. There was plenty of kindling and logs in a box beside the stove, and some matches on a shelf above his head. He recognized birch bark from his childhood reading and stuffed some into the fire-box and lit it, heaping on twigs and a log, and sat down to warm himself. The fire caught immediately, in a few minutes changing the atmosphere in the room from cold and damp to unbearably hot. He fiddled with the openings on the stove until he had muffled the roar somewhat, and then, quite suddenly, he was exhausted. He was also hungry, but the rain was still coming down heavily and he had no desire to get wet again, so he ate his last Mars bar and went to bed.

ii. A Familiar Face

At breakfast the next morning, William watched and listened. He counted about thirty workers, half of them Indian and half white. William picked a spot at the end of one of the long tables, slightly nearer to a group of white workers than to the Indians, but not so close as to imply a claim that he had earned a place at anyone's table. He relied on his memories of being a new boy in other situations to avoid breaching whatever protocol governed the proper behaviour of new camp workers.

Three or four times during the meal, Bullock appeared in the doorway to give instructions to someone, and gradually the workers drifted away until only William was left. He was wondering whether he should report for duty at the dock, when Bullock appeared and motioned to follow him. They walked up to a group of buildings near the workers' cabins, one of which turned out to be the stores. Bullock said, "Tell Rodney, the storekeeper, to give you a gallon of white paint and a brush." He pointed to a line of rocks, each about the size of a basketball, which lined the paths. "When you've done those, do the ones around the guests' cabins, then the path down to the dock, the road up to the dump, and the path to the fish hut. I'll find something else for you this afternoon."

Most of the space inside the hut was taken up with the camp supplies — beer and paint and outboard motor oil and boat cushions and paddles — but at the far end of the room, a small counter had been built across the back, behind which were kept the more stealable items: the fishing rods, lures, knives, and sweatshirts which the camp sold to the guests. A familiar figure with a wizened face waited behind the counter. "Good God," William said as he approached and focused on the individual. "R. Brown."

"Rodney," R. Brown said.

"I didn't know that."

"How could you? But you had better not call me 'Mr. Brown' in these parts."

"You're the storekeeper?"

R. Brown bowed. "Keeper of the hoard." He added, "I've been expecting you, sir."

"Me, or just some new man?"

"You. I overheard Harry at supper telling someone that we had a new man with us who called himself a college president. A wit, Harry seemed to think. Then I overheard your name and realized what fate had done. He said he was going to bring you into the stores first thing, and here we are."

"What are you doing here?"

"Working for my living. I was born not far from here, in a small town called Dryden. If you ever visit Dryden, you will understand why the first thing I can remember thinking was how I wanted to leave as soon as possible. But I return every summer to spend a weekend in Dryden and the rest of the summer here. You see, when I was a child I spent all my time reading, whatever Dryden had to offer. My father was a kindly man and didn't beat me when he caught me reading, as you might have expected in Dryden, but he did make me learn something useful. He taught me how to repair small motors — gasoline engines, outboard motors, lawnmowers, and such. 'Son,' he said, 'A man who can service small motors will never go hungry.' You see, Father lived all his life in Dryden, where small motors are ubiquitous. In the city, the ability to service small motors is not so highly regarded, but my father's advice still seemed essentially sound, so I switched to large motors, and enrolled at Van Horne. In order to earn enough money for the winter, I am obliged to return each year to where I am needed. I fulfil Harry's requirements for a storekeeper-mechanic perfectly. I can read, I can write, and I can keep the outboard motors running. Now, what about you? I think we had better drop the 'university president' label; let Harry continue to think you were joking. Let's just say . . ."

The door opened at the other end of the hut. "One gallon of white paint, one brush. Sign here," R. Brown said, loudly, turning a ledger around and pointing at the place. He looked up and over William's shoulder. "Guess what, Harry. We know each other. We were at college together last year."

William started on the first rock, recognizing that this was a kind of test or task, but unable to guess whether he would perform it well enough to be allowed to stay. He was saved almost immediately — after he had painted three rocks — when, hearing his name shouted from the direction of the lake, he ran down to the dock, where all hands were helping unload a plane that had just arrived. After that, he painted rocks with his ears open for the sound of planes arriving. By late morning he knew he was doing what Bullock wanted, making himself useful as a kind of dogsbody.

Guests tended to arrive and depart in the mornings, he learned later, and by the afternoon the sky was empty most of the time, and then, just as he was beginning to dislike painting rocks, the planes reappeared, a few, enough to allow for a major break from rock-painting. One of them was piloted by Bullock, who presented William with a pair of bright yellow boots, and a cap with a long peak. "You're getting fried," he pointed out.

About five o'clock they stopped altogether, and he took a moment to watch the other water traffic, the boats that had been out fishing all day which started to appear across the lake, heading for home.

iii. A Man in Need

AFTER SUPPER, THE white workers disappeared, and the Indians lined the rail above the dock and chatted to each other in Ojibway. William went up to his cabin, where he found he had acquired a room-mate. A man in his sixties with a seamed face sat on the other bunk, staring at his hands. He took no notice of William, who checked the impulse to advance on him, hand extended, instead saying, "I sleep here," and pointed to his bunk.

The man tilted his head back just enough to be able to see William. "And who the fuck are you?" he asked, allowing his head to droop down at the end of the question.

"William Moodie. And who the fuck are you?" It was just like the first day at school.

The man winched his head up again until he was looking squarely at William. "Gotta drink, kid?"

As it happened, William had in his bag a small flask containing about six ounces of whisky, part of a survival kit some friends at Cambridge had presented him with at his farewell party when he had been awarded the fellowship at Simcoe, a kit consisting of all the things recommended for travel in primitive countries. The kit also contained a razor blade, two Oxo cubes, a length of fine wire for snaring rabbits, some fish hooks, water purification tablets, four matches coated with wax, and a mirror, all neatly packed into a little tin about the

size of a pack of cigarettes. The whisky had not been part of
the original kit but was added at his father's suggestion. "They
used to pour it into arrow wounds," he said. "To disinfect
them. It'll come in handy if you find yourself in a logging
camp and cut your foot off."

William recognized that his room-mate was in very great
need, and took the opportunity to ingratiate himself. He found
a small tin cup on the shelf, poured about half the whisky into
it, and handed it across to the man on the other bunk, who
swallowed the whisky like the medicine it was, responding to
it in a series of convulsive heaves as if he were swallowing a
large snake whole. "Wass that?" he asked. "Scotch?" He handed back the mug. "Not too much now."

William emptied the rest of the whisky into the cup and the
man drank it down.

The door opened and a head appeared in the gap, sniffing
the air. "Arnold," the visitor called. "Bring anything back?"

"No," the man said, without looking up.

"Lying cocksucker."

Three times in the next half-hour the scene was repeated.
Each time a head enquired if Arnold had brought anything
with him, and cursed him without passion when he said no.

"What do they want?" William asked, and then, as he realized what the answer must be, said, "Why didn't you bring
some back?"

"Because I'm on the wagon is why." He nodded to the flask
in William's hand. "Don't count that. That was just to tide me
over. Got any beer left?"

"Left from what, or when?"

"How long you bin here, kid?"

"I came yesterday."

"Ah, so nobody's told you. Bunch of pricks."

The man explained. The camp workers were allowed to draw two bottles of beer a night from the stores. Enough to put out a small fire but not start a new one.

William said, "Shall I go and draw mine now? We could have one each."

"That would be terrific." The man leaned against the wall and closed his eyes.

"But if you're on the wagon, perhaps I shouldn't . . ."

"Beer doesn't count. Hurry up, for Christ's sake. The store-keeper closes up at eight."

R. Brown was just in the process of locking up, but he issued William his ration of beer, and suggested that he come back later, to the back door, and the two of them could share another bottle or two.

When William returned to his cabin, he handed a bottle to his new room-mate and watched most of it disappear at a swallow.

"Who are you?" William asked.

"Arnold's the name. Arnold Banting." He pointed to the flask. "That's it, eh?"

William upended the flask to show its emptiness, poured a little of his beer into the tin cup for himself and gave the rest of his bottle to Banting, who drank it down. The dregs disposed of, Banting said, "We'll have a little chat tomorrow," rolled himself into his blanket, and went to sleep.

William arranged his bedding so that he could climb into bed easily in the dark, turned out the light, and made his way back to the store.

"I like to read in the evenings, but it's difficult to do that in a room with three snoring, eructating guides who want the lights out at nine. So Harry let me move in here."

"Here" was a very cosy little chamber at the end of the stores, equipped with a tiny fridge, a hot-plate, a bed, and two comfortable chairs. A small radio was playing jazz music very quietly. "Now, what would you like to know?"

"Where am I?"

R. Brown decanted the rest of his bottle of beer and adjusted himself as if for the camera. "For those who can afford it," he began, "Loon Lake Lodge is known as one of the best fishing camps in North America. The quality of the fishing, for northern pike, pickerel, lake trout, and small-mouth bass, is superb; the accommodation posing as simple, is, in fact, luxurious; and the ambience, fifty miles from the nearest road in the Northern Ontario bush, is that of the frontier." He stood up and began walking up and down the room, in good lecturing style. "After a week at the lodge, guests feel they have seen the real Canadian bush, untouched since the last fur traders passed this way *en route* from Montreal to Winnipeg. All the guests are Americans, of course, from the mercantile classes — you wouldn't catch Canadians paying Bullock's prices — and thus very gullible outside the city. And so, during the day, they fish in an area so uninhabited that it still defies search parties when a bush plane crashes, but at night the camp awaits them, each log cabin equipped with a Jacuzzi tub and three-speed showers. The menu in the dining room is not elaborate, but the cook is a professional whose only flaw is that he requires three days off every month, three days which he spends in a hotel room in bed with a practical nurse, drinking and ordering room-service meals until his money runs out, when he returns to the lodge. At these times, Bullock's wife takes over the kitchen and the guests eat steak alternately with fried chicken." R. Brown turned his head as the radio program changed, then looked at his watch. "I wonder what he has in mind for you?"

"Rock painting, so far."

"I think that's temporary. A sort of initiation. After that there's rock crushing. It's after *that* that I'm curious about. Bullock might surprise us. He's a great judge of character. And now you'll have to go, I'm afraid, sir. I'm expecting a visitor."

"You shouldn't keep calling me 'sir,' you know. There's no need, anyway."

"Only in private, sir. It reassures me that this . . ." — he waved his hand around the room — "is all temporary, that one day soon we shall be back where we belong in the real world of Van Horne."

"Not me, Rodney."

"Ah. Right. I was forgetting. Tactless of me." There was a knock at the door. "Go out through the store, would you, sir? Just pull the door shut after you."

Walking down the path, William picked up a tiny breath of perfume, and guessed who R. Brown's visitor must be. The only woman in the camp, except for Bullock's wife, was the hostess in the guests' dining room.

iv. Rocks and Stones

THE NEXT DAY William painted rocks and unloaded planes, and in the evening shared his two beers with Arnold, who drank his own two walking back from the store. On the third day, all the rocks lining all the paths in the camp had been painted by noon and Bullock put him to work on the rock crusher, as R. Brown had predicted. This was a machine the size of a small concrete mixer which smashed rocks into gravel. It generated a thick cloud of rock dust, covering the operator, who had to keep it fed, and periodically spat out a tiny shard of rock that inflicted a small, deep cut on his face until William learned to work with his back to the mouth of the machine. It was incredibly noisy and in every way much harder, physically, than painting, for after the rocks were crushed, the gravel had to be shovelled into a wheelbarrow and pushed fifty yards over rough ground to where it could be loaded onto the trailer of the jeep. It was very much as William imagined it would be in a penitentiary.

His room-mate, Arnold Banting, commiserated with him for getting the worst job in camp, but confirmed R. Brown's information that it was a job everyone had to do. Anyone who refused was shipped back to town. In fact, William was finding some pleasure this early in discovering that he could stand it, for a while, at least. He tried to explain this to R. Brown, who urged him to keep his enthusiasm under control. "It makes you sound like Lawrence of Arabia saying how much you like being flogged."

William had now figured out how the camp worked. Guests arrived from as far away as Florida and were assigned cabins and guides. Each guide had his own fibreglass twelve-foot dinghy with a ten-horsepower motor, and in this he took out two guests each day. They had to be ready by seven-thirty, when the guests appeared from their breakfast, ready to go fishing. The guides were the aristocrats among the camp workers. Even the guests who treated all the other workers like plantation serfs deferred to their own guides, because only they possessed the arcane knowledge, the craft secrets that made them the equal of anyone in their boat, knowledge that could take the guest into the heart of the bush and come back with a boatload of fish. Arnold was a senior guide, so well established in his role that he did nothing else when he wasn't guiding, idling on idle days while lesser guides were expected to help out on the loading dock.

Every morning Bullock pounded on the doors of the workers' cabins at five-thirty. William got up immediately and was washed and breakfasted by six. Bullock's first priority was to get his guests out on to the lake; he was not interested in William, and no one wanted to hear the rock-crusher that early. Thus William created some time for himself to watch the guides get ready.

As each guide came down from the dining room, he detoured past the store to pick up a wooden box, about the size of an army footlocker, which he stowed under the seat in the middle of his boat. Then he filled one or two five-gallon gas tanks, packed a large pail with beer and ice, cleaned up the boat and made it ready for the guests. That done, he went up to the guests' cabin to find out what time his party wanted to go out. (Some of the guests were already hanging over the rail waiting, but the guides did not go out until seven-thirty.) Much of this was heavy work, and if the guide was late from his own breakfast, completed at a dead run. As fifteen guides competed for access to the gas pump, and to use the single ramp up to the shore to carry supplies back and forth, the activity looked to William like a scene Brueghel might have painted, called *Morning* or some such. Brueghel would certainly have included the two or three guides, like Arnold, who spent the first few minutes pacing around the dock trying to find someone who still had a bottle of beer left from the previous day, something to cut down the glare of the lake under the early-morning sun. At seven-thirty the fleet of fishing boats headed out in ones and twos, and by eight o'clock the dock was empty.

William crushed rock for two days, then, on the afternoon of the third day, Bullock told him to get ready to take out a party of two the next morning. William thought that perhaps the covering of rock dust and dried blood on his face was so thick that Bullock had mistaken him for a real guide, but Bullock confirmed that he knew who he was talking to by telling him to get Arnold to help him find a boat. "Fred Colby's in town," Bullock said. "Use his. I'll find you a permanent one later. Wash that shit off your face first."

But as he ran down to the dock to find Arnold half an hour later, Bullock called to him to cancel the plan: the guests weren't arriving after all. "Stick around, though," Bullock said. "I've got a load of supplies coming in on the next plane." He started to walk up the road.

William overtook him as he was walking up to the dining room. "Could that happen again?" he asked.

"What?"

"Asking me to guide."

"Sure. That's what I hired you for, for when I get busy. Round about now."

That night, after supper, William consulted R. Brown.

Brown said, "I was wondering if it might come to this. Have you talked to Harry about yourself at all?"

"Not since the first day."

"He probably thinks you're from around here, like me. Sioux Lookout, perhaps."

"Do I sound as if I'm from Sioux Lookout?"

"You sound like what you are. You haven't acquired any protective coloration at all. But Harry's an American himself, you see. He can't tell the difference."

"What am I going to do?"

"You like it here at Loon Lake, sir?"

"I've never been so happy in my life."

"Then we shall have to go to work." He rubbed his hands. "This could be a lark," he said. "Do you know anything about guiding, the bush?" He waved a hand in the direction of the lake.

"I have never even been in one of the boats."

"What about fishing?"

"Oh, I know all about that."

R. Brown listened carefully as William explained how each Sunday as a boy, he and two or three friends used to cycle from Raynes Park to Hampton Court, where they fished in the Thames for roach, and dace, and gudgeon, and perch, sometimes catching a dozen fish weighing several ounces each. For bait they used maggots, or bread made into a paste and rolled into little balls. When they got home, they gave their catch to the cat.

"This is a little bit different," R. Brown said. "Have you ever used an outboard motor?"

"No."

"You've seen the fish they catch here?"

"I've noticed how big they are."

"But they all look alike to you?"

"Yes."

R. Brown searched for a starting-point. "Can you swim?" he asked finally.

"Do I have to go in after them?"

"I just wanted to know if you should wear a life jacket. The guests would find it strange. Let's go. Fish first, I think."

He led William to the ice-house where the day's catch was stored. Inside, he reached into a bin and held up a large fat fish, about three feet long. "A pickerel," he said. He held up another, and another. Then he held up another that looked slightly different.

"That looks slightly different," William said.

"Good. What about this?"

They stayed in the ice-house until they were thoroughly chilled and William could identify, more or less at sight, the major species of fish that were caught in Loon Lake. Now they returned to the store and R. Brown led them around to the back, where several outboard motors in different stages of repair were clamped to a wooden beam supported by two trestles. The storekeeper hooked one of them up to a gas tank, pushed a small lever, pulled a cord, and the motor came to life. He explained what he had done, and William practised the movements until he was sure of them.

"That," R. Brown said, "Is all we can do on land. Now let us see Arnold."

Arnold said, "You want me to teach you a lifetime's experience in an hour?"

"Yes."

"There's a fee," R. Brown said, producing a case of twelve bottles of beer.

Arnold held out his hand for a bottle, banged off the cap against the edge of the bunk, and took a deep swallow. "Let's go, then."

He led the way to the dock and climbed into the middle of his boat, leaving William to steer. R. Brown joined half a dozen Indian guides who leaned over the rail to watch. "Start her up," Banting said.

William started the motor.

"Let's go."

He put the motor in gear and accelerated. The boat acted as if it had been violently kicked.

"Better untie her," Arnold said, pointing to the rope that secured the boat to the dock.

William untied the boat, and restarted the motor. They roared across the lake, out of control. Arnold made twisting motions with his hand to show William how to decrease the speed, and soon they were puttering gently towards the other shore.

"Now open it up and head for that clump of trees across the lake. Slow down when you get there."

As they approached, a gap in the trees became a channel into the next lake. "Slow down, for Christ's sake. Now. Stop the motor and drop that rock over the side. That's called your anchor. Right. Let me finish this beer and I'll tell you all about it and you'll forget and fuck up on your first day out, then I'll tell you again, and you'll get there in the end." He delivered a lecture on how to catch and net the four kinds of fish they were likely to encounter, including the northern pike, which you did not net because for some reason it lay alongside the boat when caught and you could lift it out "by the ears" and "guests have never seen that trick so they're liable to be impressed the first time you do it. Now, all you need to know else is how to fillet pickerel, how to cook shore-lunch, and where to find the fish, but that'll do for tonight. Jesus Christ, there's guys on their way from Texas right now, big bastards who've made a fortune pumping mud into drill holes who are looking forward to having you show them where the fish are up in Canada."

The next night Arnold took him out again and William began to feel slightly more comfortable in the boat. Guiding obviously took more skill than teaching Business Correspondence, but in the beginning there were parallels. You mugged up enough the night before to last you the following day, and you continued to do that until you realized you already knew enough to get through the day without sitting up at night. If he could get three or four lessons from Arnold he should be ready the next time Bullock tapped him. But two days later, Bullock assigned him to go out the following morning with a party of six, who were arriving late that afternoon. That night he got another lesson from Arnold.

v. The Guide

THE FOLLOWING MORNING he did everything he had watched the other guides do. He picked up a wooden box from the store (it contained all the materials for cooking shore-lunch, along with the dishes and pots and pans), filled his gas tank, checked with his guests to see if they wanted beer in the boat, then filled a large pail with ice from the fish hut and put in twelve bottles of beer. When his guests arrived he got them seated, and fiddled about until Arnold was ready, then followed him out on to the lake.

All day he chugged along in the wake of his room-mate. His guests were experienced fishermen and he watched them closely to see how it was done, and at shore-lunch he trotted about like Arnold's servant. He answered his guests' questions about the camp and the environment politely, cryptically, out of fragments of conversation he had overheard between other guides and their guests. As for himself, he said, in the winter he worked for a lumber company. Not a lumberjack, exactly; more on the ground, really.

There was an awkward moment in the early afternoon when one of the guests expressed some curiosity about his accent. R. Brown had enjoyed concocting a story for him to have ready to the effect that his Cambridge-cockney accent was the result of his father having come out from the old country, married a deaf and dumb girl, become a trapper and raised the boy in a remote cabin, so that the only accent William had heard from the time he was two was his father's. But he need not have worried. His guests were from Kansas and they were intrigued by what they took to be a pure Canadian dialect.

Late in the afternoon, when it was time to go home, William looked up and realized that Arnold's boat had gone, and that he was alone on the lake. Arnold was only fifty yards away, behind an island, his motor silent, paddling his boat along the shore, looking for bass, but he might as well have disappeared into the next province. William was hopelessly lost.

"Let's go," one of his guests said.

"Not yet," William said. "About now the big pike start hitting."

For another hour he paddled them along the shore, straining his ears for the sound of a friendly outboard motor.

"They ain't hitting today," the guest said. "Now can we go?"

William slowly pulled up his anchor, tidied the boat, started the motor (missing the opportunity to flood it and stall for a little time, a trick Arnold showed him that night), and moved slowly out into the middle of the lake to look for the way home. He crossed the lake to what looked like a channel but which after ten minutes turned into a blind bay, and he had to come out.

"Harry asked us to make sure the shore-lunch spots were tidy," he said. "That's a popular spot, right there."

"Looks as clean as a whistle to me," the guest said. "Could we go home, please? Like, before dark?"

Now William headed across the lake in a wide curve, peering down as if looking for submerged rocks, then on the other side two boats appeared, clearly purposefully headed for home, and William nodded to the guest. "Sure," he said. "If you've had enough, that is."

Bullock came to the cabin that evening to tell him that he was shifting him to another party, one of three guides looking after six men from Wisconsin. The other two guides were brothers, Indians, Eddie and Joe Goose.

Bullock said, "The guys you had today complained that you kept them out too long. They asked for someone a bit less gung-ho."

When Bullock had gone, Arnold suggested that it was time for William to get his beer ration.

William said, "I still have seven bottles left from what I took out today. In my boat."

Arnold rolled off his bunk. "I was thinking," he said. "Maybe it would be a good time for me to show you a bit of the geography. If you hadn't got lost you would've been all right today. The way you got out of it was right clever, but they're not all assholes who come up here."

It took an hour and a half for William to drink a beer and Arnold to dispose of the other six. By that time, they had visited all the main fishing spots within a mile of the camp, and then it was dusk and time for William to pick up his two beers before the store closed. Back in the cabin, Arnold, his second (or eighth) bottle of beer opened, said, "You know, I think I'm going to beat it this time. I haven't had a drop of liquor for a week."

All day, William never let Eddie Goose out of his sight. He assisted effectively enough at shore-lunch, and then in the afternoon as he was trolling close to the shore, his propeller hit a rock and the motor started to scream. William shut the motor down.

"You've sheared a pin," his guest, a dermatologist from Minneapolis, said. "I do it all the time back home."

William took out his paddle and guided them in to the shore, while he thought. He said, "You know how to fix it?"

The dermatologist looked surprised. "Sure, but . . ."

William said. "I've got something cutting into my foot. These are my new boots. I don't want to use up your fishing time, so if you'd like to fix the pin, I'll just have a look at my foot."

The dermatologist laughed. "Maybe I should look at your foot. Okay, throw me a shear-pin."

William began to pat his pockets, wondering what a shear-pin looked like.

"You've got one in your tackle box," the guest said, pointing to the metal box that R. Brown had lent him, complete with a few lures and other odds and ends, to help out with his disguise. "I saw it when you got the bottle-opener."

William had not touched the box so far except to find the opener. Now he lifted the box close to the guest, opened the lid, and immediately caught his finger on a hook, giving time and room for the dermatologist to lift out a small steel pin about an inch long and toss it in his hand.

"Go ahead," he said. William climbed ashore and sat where he could watch the dermatologist from under the peak of his cap, while he took off his boot and sock. He bathed his foot and when the doctor's back was turned made a small cut in the ball of his foot with a piece of flint, smearing the resultant few drops of blood over the sole of his foot to show the dermatologist when he was finished with the motor. "Stone in my boot," he said. "I'll put a Band-Aid on it. You finished?" He bandaged the wound, put his sock and boot back on, and they resumed fishing.

That night William learned that his guests had had to return to Minneapolis unexpectedly. Now he was to help out with a large party of salesmen, winners of a competition set up by a piston ring manufacturer. Already he was feeling confident enough to be able to cope with two piston ring salesmen. He knew the fish, more or less. He identified all medium-sized birds as fish-ducks, and small ones as yellow-bellied sapsuckers. Of large birds that hovered, he used a comment he had learned from Eddie Goose: "Not too many of them left." And he kept the huge peak of his hat well down, covering his face, which gave him time to compose a reply for trickier questions. When he explained this to R. Brown, the store keeper said, admiringly, "A system, yet!"

There were twelve salesmen, needing six boats and six guides, and most of them knew nothing about fishing. The two in William's boat dangled their lines in the water, indifferent to what they might catch, handing William the rod if they did get a bite. They were there only because they had won a prize; from their conversation it was clear they would have preferred to spend the week in one of several brothels they knew of in Central America. But they were exactly what William needed. The tiny knowledge he had so far acquired, spread very thin, was adequate to the task of guiding them. They did not fish for long. At first one or two, then more than half of the salesmen, including the two in William's boat, announced that they would rather play poker than sit in a boat in the middle of the lake, "getting fried," and William found himself being paid to do nothing. For as long as the ring salesmen were at the camp, he had to stand by for the call to go fishing, but they assured him that they had no intention of going out in his boat again, and suggested he join the poker game. He used the opportunity to approach Eddie Goose, offering him half-a-day's pay in return for a guided tour of the lake and river system.

"Secrets known only to the Indians?" Eddie asked. "Sure. You got any beer in your boat?"

That afternoon Eddie showed him six more places to catch pickerel, one good bay to cast for northern pike, and an island where smallmouth bass nested along the shore. It was like being shown the places to shop for bargains in an unfamiliar town.

On the second afternoon that he went out with Eddie Goose while the guests played cards, William remembered four of the fishing spots he had been shown the day before, and was reminded of the rest. On the third day he remembered every spot and found his own way home. Suddenly the area which had seemed vast, strange, almost unknowable, was reduced to the status of a watery village with a handful of side streets and one major road linking it to the next village. By the time the salesmen had left, William had learned enough about fishing and guiding from Eddie and Arnold to satisfy almost anyone he was likely to get in his boat, and he never got lost again. Only on those rare days when the fish weren't biting did he still find himself cruising the major channels, looking for Eddie Goose or Arnold, a real guide, to tell him what to do.

There was one more test. Early in June, on the third day with the same party, Bullock told him he was flying out the next day for trout. Arnold explained what this meant. "There are good trout lakes all round," he said, "but you can only get to them with a plane. Harry keeps a few aluminum canoes at these lakes, and you have to take a little light outboard motor — Rodney will give you one — your lunch-box, and everything else you need for the day. When you get there, you find the canoe and go fishing."

In the event, William was not alone: four men were to fish for trout that morning and another guide joined him in loading the plane with the supplies and hoisting their guests on board. They flew out and landed, and the other guide opened the door, stepped on to the float, and jumped ashore as soon as they had taxied close enough. He tied the float to a tree and waited for William to hand him the supplies, which he managed without incident. Then the pilot said, "You go on down and help these guys out. I'll steady them up here."

It was a repeat of the first day. William had watched closely as the other guide had stepped on to the float and jumped to the shore, and now he followed, disappearing through a light covering of bush into six feet of ice-cold water.

But the sun was hot enough to dry him out by noon, and they caught a lot of trout, and the guests admired him for his stoicism, assuming it was a local characteristic. "Fucking guy's soaking wet," one guest said to the other. "Doesn't give a fuck, though. Guess they're used to it."

vi. A Rush of Desire

ALL THROUGH JUNE, William concentrated on getting his impersonation right. By the end of the month his face and hands were black, but when he took off his cap a clean line separated the white-skinned Englishman from the newly minted Canadian guide. He had learned enough about his trade to provide his guests with a different fishing experience every day for five days. Guests who stayed longer found that on day six they were fishing in the same places and for the same fish as on day one, but almost no one noticed. To those who did, and remarked on it, William said he had brought them back here because he had heard the fishing was pretty good "up at the falls" the day before, which usually meant that the fish would move down to where they now were the next day. It was something like he had heard Arnold say in similar circumstances. By the end of the month he could catch, clean, and cook fish on request; respond to routine questions; and safely confess ignorance of all others.

The guests were keen to treat him with respect, even deference, admiring his knowledge of the geography and the wildlife, and envying his lifestyle, which they were paying a very large sum to imitate for a few days. Once, after some guests had left, Bullock told William that he had just guided two of the chief mobsters from Duluth, part of a very large group that had come together from all over the midwest to chat together away from the hurly-burly of the cities; and just to be sure they had really escaped from civilization, they chose their own site for shore-lunch, then sent the guides out on the lake after the meal while they had a chat. They talked until sunset, when they waved the guides back. The next morning the party broke up and William's pair gave him two hundred dollars, all their brand new fishing tackle, which they hadn't bothered to unwrap, and the largest bottle of whisky William had ever seen. From this he refilled his little emergency flask and tucked the rest into the bottom of his bag under his bunk. It would, he reasoned, be irresponsible to let Arnold know about it in his delicate condition; on the other hand, he had learned, not just from Arnold's example, that at Loon Lake under certain circumstances half a gallon of whisky was the hardest currency a man could have.

No one else questioned his accent. When the guests did speculate about William, after they had admired and envied him sufficiently, it was from the perspective of people who sent their own sons to law school and believed he was wasting his life. William saw it in their eyes, overheard them at shore-lunch, and knew that he would be getting advice before they left. The camp, the wonderful fishing, the simple life, all moved them to an access of sympathy with their fellow man, and they offered their help and advice. Most typically, they would seek him out on the last evening, ask him to come to the cabin, give him a larger tip than they had budgeted for (though never as big as the gangsters' tip), and urge him to think of making something of himself, even give him their cards.

William did not actively encourage their concern. His need to avoid the truth had caused him to construct a simple story, which he polished with each repetition. He was born nearby, he told them (later changed to "not far up-river"). He'd done a lot of things, but nothing suited him like guiding. In the winter he "cut pulp" — worked for a logging company that harvested the local timber to make pulp for paper. In between he lived with his folks, in town. He wasn't married, but he did have a girlfriend who worked as a cook at another camp.

By July he almost believed the story himself.

As far as the camp workers were concerned, he allowed it to be known that he had left Toronto for personal reasons. They understood this to mean that he was wanted by the police, or by someone who wanted to hurt him, or that he was being pursued for support payments by a wife, all of which were familiar to them. It had been obvious to all of them from his arrival that he would not be guiding if he did not have something to conceal.

At the end of July, William looked like a deeply contented man as he led his guests expertly from lake to lake, carrying out his part of Bullock's promise that it was the best fishing camp in eastern Canada. And certainly he felt enough at home among the lakes and rocky shores of this tiny corner of the Canadian wilderness that for the rest of his life the spring brought an urge to return. But his successful impersonation of a guide gave him room to relax a bit, which brought a reawakened consciousness and made him aware that, now that he had discovered this world, it could only be temporary for him. For more than two months he had been happy not to read a word. Each day his whole energy had been absorbed by the need to play his part successfully, and after supper he had been content to drink a bottle of beer and eat a chocolate bar, sitting on the dock as the sun went down, before he rolled himself into his blankets at nine o'clock. But now that he had experienced the reality behind the page, he felt the stirring of old needs, the first of which was a desire to eat a meal in a restaurant, reading a magazine, and this brought a rush of desire for his books and all those magazines that specialized in literary gossip, the English specialist's equivalent of the tabloids. Loon Lake had been a very important period in his life, but it was not a resting place.

And yet he did not feel quite ready to go. In some sense, he did not feel that he had yet earned the right to move on. He felt rather as he did when his fellowship had not been renewed, and then again, when he was fired from Van Horne, that he had still not had the experience he had come for, and he didn't want to go home without it. He had seen this world, and he had successfully imitated an inhabitant of it, but he had not lived it, really. Perhaps it was not his to live; perhaps he was a hundred years too late.

And besides, there was Gloria. He had written to everybody he knew in his first week at Loon Lake, and had got a fairly immediate reply from Gloria to the effect that it would be agreeable to resume their correspondence. "Do you remember," she had written, "the night we saw *Hiroshima, Mon Amour*? The film society brought it here last week." No signal could have been clearer or better received.

Some of this he tried to explain to Harry Bullock two days later, as they ate the meal he had prepared, and waited for someone to rescue them.

vii. Lost

BULLOCK HAD APPROACHED William to come with him for a plane ride. August was a slow month at the lodge. Serious fishermen came in the spring and fall. In August, the rates went down, and a few married couples appeared. The guides called them tourists because they were attracted by Bullock's advertisements in the town paper, and despised them for their ignorance and their poverty. Still, half the cabins were empty, and thus Bullock's invitation was welcome because during slack periods guides as junior as William reverted to crushing rock, and now that he was a guide, he felt the indignity of doing chores with all the strength of feeling of a native big-game hunter being asked to do a spell as houseboy.

"I've got to take a canoe over to One Man Lake," Bullock said. "There's good trout there in the fall. And I want to take a look around, see where the rest of the canoes are."

There was no question of anyone stealing the canoes that Bullock parked at the outlying trout lakes; only the Indians knew the land well enough to do that successfully, and since most of the Indians in the local band worked for Bullock, he was immune from theft. But trees could fall on them, moose could step through the bottoms of them, and they could be blown off the shore to float half a mile away, and thus need to be returned to the place that had been established as the safest landing place. "Bring your lunch-box and a couple of rods," Bullock said. "You can show me how it's done."

They took off into a greying sky and flew ten miles north as the grey turned to black. "It's not supposed to do this," Bullock said, as the first lightning fractured the sky. He wheeled the plane round and flew at right-angles to his previous course. The storm knocked the little Norseman across the sky, and Bullock had to struggle to pull it back on course. They continued like this for about fifteen minutes, then Bullock said, "Jesus Christ" as the air disappeared from under them and they dropped heavily sideways towards the lake below. "Hang on," Bullock shouted, and did something to make their turn sharper, but also pulled them on to an even keel, and then one wing touched the lake and the plane vaulted across the surface. They struck a small reef, bounced into deeper water, and settled quickly more than half under, the engine steaming.

William lifted his head and tested himself for wholeness. He had been sitting on the floor of the plane, thinking about Gloria, using an old coat for a cushion. The final impact had thrown him across the plane and rolled him around the floor like a piece of unsecured cargo, coming to rest wedged against the wall of the plane, hemmed in by his own lunch-box. He had been lucky: the lunch-box had not been tied down; it weighed at least seventy-five pounds and one corner of it could have crushed his ribs, or broken a leg bone, but its attempts to smash him had been thwarted by the metal ribs of the floor, and thus instead of damaging him, it had possibly saved him from injury by creating a niche for him to lie in. He pushed the box away and scrambled free, stumbling to his knees on the sloping floor.

Bullock had not been as lucky. Although he had been buckled into his seat, the frame of the seat had been torn free of its moorings, and he lay on his side, still strapped in, his eyes closed.

William crawled forward just as Bullock regained consciousness. "Untie me," Bullock said, his face white. He closed his eyes.

William unbuckled him and dragged the seat away, then struggled to get him into a sitting position, but as he lifted him, Bullock screamed, then said immediately, in a more or less normal voice, "Don't pull that one. I think she's broke." He reached across his body with his left arm and lifted his right wrist. "Broke it is," he said. "Up at the top. I felt it go, like someone stepping on piece of firewood."

The plane lifted slightly, then settled perceptibly lower. "We'll have to disembark, if that's the word," Bullock said. "The wind's catching that wing. Come around the other side of me and see if you can do what you was trying to do before from that side. Sit me up."

Bullock was heavy, but their three good arms got him upright and sitting against the wall of the plane, where William joined him. The storm seemed worse. "There's no water in the plane," Bullock said. "Are we on a reef?"

William crawled forward into the cabin and raised himself until he could see the lake through the side window. At first he could not make sense of what he was looking at until he realized that part of the window was itself under water, and they were sitting below the waterline. Water was trickling in at a dozen places and soon a major leak would develop and the plane would fill up. If they were currently resting on the bottom of the lake, or on a reef, then there might be a space left with air in it right at the front, but they could not count on it. They would have to get out now, and to do that they would have to open the door and fill the plane with water. William crawled higher into the cockpit and looked out again. Now he thought his eye was above the level of the lake, although the wind shifted the surface so much that he had to wait several minutes to be sure. Then he saw the shore, which was very close, no more than twenty feet away, and he worked out that a very few feet from the plane there was probably room to stand and, the second bit of luck, that the wind was blowing off the shore so there were no waves at the edge.

The plane shifted slightly, but only seemed to settle more firmly in the same place, and William saw a ridge of rock appear for a moment in a trough of the waves, appear and disappear, and he guessed that the plane was now resting solidly on a reef, so he had time to think.

I am in a plane that has crashed in a lake during a storm, he thought, *somewhere in Northern Ontario. The pilot has a broken arm. So far there is not much water in the plane, because the pressure of the water outside is keeping the door shut, but the skin of the fuselage is only canvas, and at any moment we are going to fill up, so I have to get us out as soon as I can, if I can.*

He crawled back to Bullock, who was sitting on the floor, propped against the side of the plane. "We've got to get out," he told him.

"Swim?" Bullock pointed to his broken arm. "Sidestroke?"

"The shore is quite close, only twenty feet away. I think if we can get across the first ten feet then we can walk ashore."

"How about the early bit? That ten feet you keep talking about."

"Here's what I think we might do." He outlined his scheme. "You go first."

"I think I have to, don't I?"

William set about the first part of the plan. He dragged Bullock's seat into place in the centre of the cabin, in line with the door, and jiggled it around until it felt wedged. Next, step by step, he gathered up everything loose in the cabin, tool-boxes, rolls of tarpaulin, clothing — everything except his shore lunch-box — and piled it around and on top of the seat. Last he put the wooden box on top of the pile. The top edge of the box wedged neatly under the headrest. The whole thing looked to him like a bonfire pile awaiting its Guy Fawkes. He crawled back down to Bullock and got him seated on a small flat boat cushion, facing the nose of the plane. Lifting himself with his legs, supported by his good arm, Bullock inched back-wards towards the pile as William moved the cushion under him. When they reached the pile, Bullock looked around and up at the lunch-box. "I have to climb on that?" he asked.

"I can't see another way."

"Let's go, then. There's a bit of water in here now."

Together they got Bullock seated on top of the box.

"Look out the window," William said. "Where is the surface of the water in relation to your eye?"

"If it were in here I'd be up to my neck."

"Don't duck your head when you go through the door."

William had found a coil of rope for the last step. He tied one end around his own waist and thought about the best place to secure the other. "If it gets tangled when you go through the door," he said, "you don't want to be tied to it."

"You done this before, kid?"

"I read about it somewhere." William tied the rope to the handle of the lunch-box. "That should do it. The thing is for you to have something to hang on to, but something you can let go of if you have to. All set?"

"This is the interesting bit."

William climbed up the pile beside Bullock, as high as he could get and still be able to get the door open. He stretched his leg out and pushed down on the door handle with his boot, forcing the door open a crack, and the water poured in. It took longer than he thought it would, but in a short time the bottom of the plane was full of water; the level climbed steadily up the door, equalizing the pressure on both sides, and the door opened wide and the level climbed more rapidly as William scrambled close to the top of the pile. Bullock had gauged it right. When the water stopped coming in, it just reached his shoulders.

"I'm not sure how long I've got," Bullock said. "That water's cold. Funny things are happening inside my head."

William measured the distance to the door. There was enough room to keep his head above water as he went through, but if he stumbled climbing over the sill he could get into trouble. He launched himself at the opening, submerging as he went through the door and surfacing outside the plane, swimming a few strokes until his feet found bottom. He walked forward until he was balanced, the water just below his waist now, then he turned, pulled the rope taut, and called to Bullock.

Bullock appeared in the doorway, apparently standing on the sill, holding on to the rope with his good arm. He pulled himself along the rope one-handedly, until William could grab him and help him for the last few yards, stumbling with him up to the shore, laying him down on the slope of the rock, almost unconscious. William started to untie the rope around his waist, then walked back into the lake until the water was up to his chest, and jerked and pulled the rope this way and that until the lunch-box appeared bobbing in the doorway.

Pulling down hard, he got the two corners of the box through the door, then towed it to the shore.

viii. Survival

BULLOCK'S FACE WAS the same ancient grey colour as the rock he was lying on and his eyes were closed. William turned his attention to finding some way to get them sheltered from the rain. First he searched his jacket for the little survivor kit that he still carried and found the tiny flask of whisky. He poured a trickle into Bullock's mouth. Bullock coughed in text-book fashion and opened his eyes. William canted the flask and let Bullock sip it down at his own pace. He drank about half the whisky, closed his eyes, and opened them full. "Like getting shipwrecked with fucking Robinson Crusoe," he said.

The rain streamed down. There was a groundsheet in his lunch-box, to wear when guiding in the rain, and for guests to sit on during shore-lunch. William retrieved it and set about finding two young trees the right distance apart, with flat ground between them. When he had established a site, he used his filleting knife to cut a length of the rope to make a ridge pole. He draped the groundsheet across the rope, and cut another length of rope, unravelling it for the thin cords he wanted to tie the corners of the groundsheet to nearby branches. That done he half-supported, half-dragged Bullock under cover, his back against the lunch-box, and tackled the problem of a fire.

He foraged where the trees were thickest, finding even after the storm an occasional few square inches of dryness, and he gathered the pine cones and twigs he needed for the beginning. After that, a bit of dampness would probably not matter, and he continued gathering larger and wetter pieces of kindling until he was breaking up dead branches with his boot. When the pile was waist high, he chose a spot just outside the canopy, up against a small rock wall, then sat down with his survivor kit. None of the four matches could be wasted — in better times he had seen guides use half a box to light a single fire — and to make sure of spares he slit each match in two with the razor blade. First with the razor blade, then with the filleting knife, he created a pile of kindling, beginning with tiny shavings, moving on to toothpick-sized slivers, then to a pile of matchsticks, and finally to a heap of thin whole twigs, a pile as big as his head. He laid out the wood that he would follow with, graded to size. He figured he had only one chance that night. He had created plenty of matches, but the careful preparations had taken so long that there might not be enough light to start again. The storm was not abating at all, so there would simply be no way to forage for another load of dry material. He looked around for a good striking surface, eventually settling on his filleting knife, polished it hard to get rid of dampness, and struck the match.

One match was enough. Each size of kindling caught in succession, and when the first finger-thick twigs started to crackle he knew he had won. Although the fire was protected somewhat by the wall that formed its back, it hissed continually, but none of the wood was sodden, and the flames bit hungrily into each new stick. In fifteen minutes he had a roaring blaze, which was warming from four feet away and began to steam his clothes as he knelt to feed it. He heard a scraping noise behind him and turned to find Bullock, his eyes bright, inching his bottom forward, and he jumped to help him get close, dragging the lunch-box to prop him up. "Not Robinson Crusoe," Bullock whispered. "Fucking Aladdin."

They watched the blaze for a few minutes. Although the fire did not suffer the most direct downfall, still plenty of water hissed in the flames and William saw that it was a matter of reversing the usual aim of fire-fighting: he had to make the fire big enough to defeat the storm's attempt to quench it. He set off to find what he could in the near darkness and was alarmed when he returned twenty minutes later with an armful of wood to see how much the fire had shrunk.

"Bigger," Bullock said.

William pointed up to the canopy. There was a gap between the edge of the groundsheet and the wall, but the smoke had already blackened the edge of the canopy. A bigger fire would surely throw up flames to reach the groundsheet. Then he made another discovery. Five feet along from the fire the wall was dry, and when he looked up to see why, he saw that there was a significant overhang of rock where the wall in that place sloped outwards as it went up. There would be much less loss of combustibility from the rain here, and he set about the task of moving his fire along the wall, under the overhang. Because of the much better conditions, he soon had the new fire going, and he let the rain take care of the old one as he helped Bullock into a new position. Then the two of them were sitting comfortably, drying in front of a roaring fire whose heat was being thrown back at them by the wall. Feeling he had earned a pause, William took a sip of the whisky and handed the flask to Bullock. "One sip," he ordered, coughing.

"It's like the army," Bullock said. "The good bits."

There was a great deal of wood to be got to last them through the night: William estimated that the fire needed to consume wood at about a third of the rate at which he could gather it; if he foraged for an hour he would be able to rest for two.

Bullock said in a small but firm voice, "I don't reckon on being able to lie down, but just the weight of this sucker might be more than I can handle."

A new problem. William concentrated as hard as he could on trying to remember the contents of his Boy Scouts' First Aid Badge (Second Class). There, if he could recover them, were the instructions with a diagram on how to tie a splint. Nothing came, but the general idea was obvious. First the arm would have to be braced with some wood; then the whole thing suppported by a sling from the shoulder. He tried to remember again what the diagram looked like and felt a punch on his arm. "Wake up," Bullock said.

"I was just trying to remember something."

"You've been asleep for ten minutes."

"I'm trying to remember something." He concentrated, and this time he saw the two halves of a broomstick and the four or five neckerchiefs that were used as examples of improvisation. No such materials existed in this place.

Bullock nudged him and he opened his eyes, or rather he returned to the world, because he had not in fact closed them. "That time I thought you'd died," Bullock said. "What the fuck are you doing?"

"Concentrating." But he needed desperately to rest for a few minutes. "Can you stay awake?" he asked Bullock.

"I sure as hell can't sleep, unless you've got some morphine in that little wonderbox."

"I must have a few minutes."

"I understand. Like driving the Trans-Canada Highway in the middle of the afternoon. Take all the time you want. Make the fire up first."

He stumbled through the dim woods, gathering an armful of wood, and laid it within reach of Bullock's good arm. Then he took off his jacket, rolled it up for a pillow, and stretched out as close to the fire as he could get.

"You've had half an hour," Bullock said, when he opened his eyes next. "Stay with it. I'm good for a while."

But now his head was clear. "I'm going to fix your arm," he said.

ix. First Aid

HE MADE SURE of enough wood for the fire, then turned to the problem of splints. He had no hatchet to split logs, so he tried to find two naturally straight branches. Birch seemed to offer the best possibility because the projecting twigs broke off very close to the main stem, whereas pine twigs left behind a sharp spike that he would have to saw off with his knife. But the pieces of birch he found were all misshapen or pulpy from being too long dead, and it began to look as if he was going to have to go through a very laborious business of hacking down a young birch of the right thickness and trimming it with his knife. He circled behind Bullock into a part of the woods he had not yet tried and, as he passed the lunch-box, saw a better solution. The lid of the box was a piece of heavy plywood edged with strips of one-by-two pine to hold it rigid.

"Can you prop yourself up for about a minute?" he asked Bullock.

Bullock leaned forward and grasped his trouser leg with his good hand, and nodded. "Two minutes," he said.

William pulled the box away, opened back the lid and kicked it off its hinges. Four hard kicks smashed the edges free and, once he had flattened the projecting nails, he had the materials for splints. He dropped the wood and pushed the lunch-box back in place behind Bullock's back.

When he had cleaned the two pieces of wood, he explained to Bullock what he wanted him to do. First he had to cut about three inches off the pieces of wood, which meant cutting a deep groove around the wood and snapping off the end without splintering it. That done, Bullock had to be stood up and the thumb of his broken arm temporarily hooked into the pants pocket to keep the weight off it. William cut the arm of Bullock's shirt away from the shoulder with the razor-blade and tore the sleeve into long strips. He was relieved to find no bones projecting through the skin, but the break was obvious by the huge purple bruise that had already formed.

He was almost ready. Bullock leaned against a tree. "Any of that whisky left?" he asked. William gave him the rest, which he swallowed down. They waited ten minutes for the slight anaesthetic effect to work, and Bullock gave him the signal. As soon as he started to work it became obvious that Bullock would have to lie down. William helped him to stretch out on the fairly dry ground near the fire and, as quickly as he could, bound the wooden slats to his upper arm, pulling tight to bring the pieces of bone together. Bullock screamed, and sweat poured from his face, and he said, "I think you did it. I heard her click. I mean, Jesus Christ, who would have chosen William the Moody to be the medic when he lands in the bush with a broken arm in a storm you'd think William the Moody would be the last on the list if you had time to think but he's done pretty good so far so let's give him a chance, eh, let's hear it for Moody, you guys," and then he fainted. William guessed that he had been babbling to shout down the pain. He pulled the lunch-box into place and brought Bullock round and got him propped up again while he devised a sling of the remaining strips of his shirt, and when he had done that he had done everything he could. The two men leaned against the box, waiting for some energy to return. After an hour, William made a foray for wood, then slept for a while sitting upright. When he woke up, Bullock was watching him. William felt Bullock's forehead and was surprised to find it fairly cool; he wondered when some kind of fever would take over, and hoped that help would have arrived by then. He said, "Will they see the fire from the air? They must, surely."

"Been thinking about that. Don't look very good. See, first of all, they can't fly in a storm like this, and I've known this weather to stay for a couple of days. Let's hope not. Then, see, I told them where I was going, which ain't where we are. The lake I was heading for is ten miles southwest of the camp. I tried to fly round the storm and we are now about twenty miles north of the camp. See? First we have to wait for the storm to blow itself out, then for them to look in the wrong place before they search the whole area."

"But the plane. It's sticking out of the water. Someone should see that."

"Should. When the sun comes out and they look around the country they're bound to see it, I would think, yes, and then the smoke will tell 'em we're still alive, and then they'll have to figure how to land without hitting our plane. I figure three days. And now you've fixed me up, I'm hungry already."

"I've been thinking about that. I'd better make us something to eat."

Bullock stared at him, then followed him with his eyes as William stood to look inside the lunch-box. "I forgot what we were leaning against," Bullock said. "Did you figure on this when you tied the rope to it?"

"No, it was just a good place to tie the rope. But when I thought about cutting it off I realized that it might be useful." He was kneeling, lifting things out of the box: fry-pan, two saucepans, plates, knives, forks, spoons, salt, pepper, small packets of butter and lard, crushed corn flakes and Carnation milk for dipping and breading fish fillets, packet of coffee, sugar, can of beans, can of peas, half a loaf of sliced white bread, quarter pound of bacon, can of peaches for dessert. All a guide needed, once he had caught some fish.

"What about a bacon sandwich?"

Bullock shook his head in wonder, and William arranged a ring of stones on the edge of the fire to form a stove, and filled the circle with embers of charcoal. He kept back two slices of bacon and fried the rest. While it was frying he scrambled down to the lake for a saucepan of water, getting soaked in the process, put the pan on the edge of the fire, and hung his jacket and shirt on sticks in front of the fire while he organized their supper. Ten minutes later he had bacon sandwiches and coffee ready.

After supper the rain stopped for a while, and William gathered some more wood and made another trip to the lake to wash the pots and dishes, and to bring back some drinking water, before they settled down for the night.

Every hour he woke up cold, and made up the fire, and went back to sleep. The ground under the canopy and close to the fire was dry now, and he could stretch out. Whenever he stirred, Bullock was watching him, and then he woke and the light was streaking the sky, and Bullock finally had closed his eyes and stayed asleep as William made up the fire and assembled the equipment for making breakfast.

x. The Canoe

THE STORM, WHICH had seemed to be dying in the night, had renewed itself with the dawn, and they had to prepare for another day, and perhaps another night, before the search would begin. There were four slices of bread left, two small slices of bacon, the beans and the peas. It was time to see what the country could supply.

He took one of the fish-hooks from his survival kit and tied it to the ten-foot length of rabbit wire. He sifted the ground around his feet until he found a fragment of granite that would do for a weight, a jagged shard that he could bend into the line, and for bait he hooked on a square inch of raw bacon. This time he kept his clothes on. Naked was all right for a quick dash to the edge, but he had no idea how long he might have to spend trying to catch a fish — as long as he could stand it — and it was necessary to have some protection from the wind; even soaking-wet clothes were better than nothing. The temperature was no more than fifty degrees, and the water was cold.

In the event, he caught a fish immediately. The lake was virtually unfished. When he threw his line out, at least four fish raced to grab the bait and he hooked a three-pound pickerel. Before he retreated, he searched his pockets for a scrap of paper, rolled it into a pellet, and flicked it out on the lake; there was an immediate flurry as it disappeared, confirming that he would have no problem getting more fish.

He filleted the pickerel on the shore, and peeled off the skin. Even as he washed the fillets, the dark shapes of curious and not-yet-timid fish approached to check the disturbance. He gave himself the luxury of watching them for a few minutes until a huge northern pike flashed through the water and they disappeared. He cut a small piece of very white flesh from the throat of the pickerel to serve as future bait, and preserved it between two flat rocks where he could find it easily. He rolled up his fishing line, and turned to scramble back to the shelter, pausing first to look around the sky to see if there was any sign of a break. There was something wrong; his eyes had missed something that he was registering now. The plane was gone. The rain still obscured the clear view across the lake, but there was no doubt that he had seen it last night.

He had been guiding with Indians for two months now, and though he remained a rationalist and an agnostic, he had become interested in what he thought of as Indian legends. But he was not in a mood to take the disappearance of the plane as a sign, realizing immediately that if it was, it was only a sign that he was not quite in his right mind. The plane had simply slid deeper into the lake. This meant that the lake shelved from four feet deep to twenty, or even thirty, in a few yards. It was possible; the rock walls which fringed some of the lakes went up sometimes to forty feet, and there was no reason why the bottom of the lake should not be similarly rugged. He took the question back to Bullock, who had a better explanation. "It flipped," he said. "The wind caught the wing and turned her over, dislodged it from the reef it was on. Gives us a problem, don't it?"

"Why? The water's too cold to have tried to salvage any-thing, anyway."

"People looking for us won't see it. So when the storm clears, we have to hope they see our fire. They won't be look-ing for a fire, though. They'll be looking for a plane. We're fucked. What's for breakfast?"

"Fish."

Bullock looked at the fillets in William's hand and nodded. "Got a miniature fishing rod in that little box, I guess."

"More or less. Some hooks, anyway." William set out the corn flakes and canned milk to bread the fish. Bullock now made his first contribution. "I'd just fry them like that. Takes less fat, and we might need the canned milk."

William did as he was told, and they ate the fish with one slice of bread each. Lately, after nearly three months of fish every day, he had not been eating it at shore-lunch, contenting himself with a plate of beans and the canned peaches. Now, once more, it tasted as delicious as it had that first week of guiding. He made them some coffee, and when it was drunk, gathered up the dishes and pots for washing. Bullock said, "Don't wash the fry-pan. It'll just take up more fat next time. What fat have you got left? Hardly enough for a fry-up? Don't wash the pan, then."

William gathered some wood, and all that day they watch-ed the rain and stayed dry. Every two hours, William made a quick excursion into the trees for fuel. At noon they ate the cans of beans and peas and carrots, heated up together in a saucepan. At the end of the afternoon, William caught another pickerel, which he cut up into chunks, and, with the last slice of bacon and the Carnation milk and water, made a kind of chowder. They followed it with the can of peaches. "There's enough fat for a breakfast fry-up, but there's only half a slice of bread each left, and a bit of coffee," he said.

Late in the evening, William made them each a cup of beef bouillon from the Oxo cubes in his kit, and they settled down to wait out the night.

At dawn the rain had stopped, but the sky was still thick and grey as William made his way down to the edge of the lake to catch their breakfast. Once more he hooked a fish within moments of casting out the line. As he filleted and skinned the fish, the clouds pulled apart, and by the time he was washing his hands in the lake, half the sky was blue and the clouds that had looked so permanent were being routed. William took off his clothes, slipped shivering into the lake, and swam out to see if he could find the plane. Ten yards from the shore, a flash of silver caught his eye, coming from a part of the shore which was hidden by an outcropping of rock. He turned and swam parallel to the shore until he had rounded the little peninsula and could see that the gleam had come from the upturned prow of an aluminum canoe bobbing along at the water's edge. It was the canoe which had been tied to their floats and evidently been shaken loose when the plane turned over. William grabbed the prow and, half-walking, half-swimming, pulled it along the shore to his fishing and washing place. There he tipped the canoe over, draining it. The front and back seats concealed flotation tanks. The front one had kept the prow above water but the rear tank had been punctured through the side of the canoe, a hole the size of a dollar, and he had to tip the canoe this way and that half a dozen times to get most of the water out. When he had bailed out as much as he could, he reamed the hole with the handle of his knife, pressing back the jagged edges, until he thought he had a hole he could plug. Then he dragged the canoe up high on the shore.

He was dry now, and dressed himself reluctantly, feeling the pleasure of the sun on his skin. He washed off the fish again and prepared to return to Bullock. Before he went back he decided to test the efficacy of fish as bait, and put a small piece of the pickerel fillet on the hook and threw it in. It was snapped almost immediately by something very big and he grabbed too late as the line was stripped out of his hand and disappeared into the lake. It was the first time he had not wrapped the end of the line about his wrist, and he wondered how much his carelessness would cost them.

"The condemned man's breakfast?" Bullock asked as William threw the last bit of lard into the pan and fried the pickerel.

"They'll see us this morning."

"They might."

Confirming his words, the first search plane appeared out of the sky and made a sweep over the lake and their fire. William jumped up and waved, and the plane gave a little wig-wag in response.

("Campers?" the pilot asked the man from the Forestry department.

"I would think so. They look as though they holed up there on account of the storm."

"Smart. Those canoes are tippy sons of bitches."

"No sign of our boys, though. We're too far north."

"That's what I figure."

"Unless . . . You ever had a car go in the lake, Lou?"

"I've seen a couple."

"Driver get out all right?"

"One did, one didn't."

"Why didn't he?"

"He hit a tree first. He was concussed."

"And that was a car?"

"You figure Harry's bought it?"

"If he crashed on land, I'd bet that he'd come out of it. He's done it twice already, crawled away from the wreck. But we haven't been able to find the plane, which means to me that it's under water."

"With Harry and that Moodie guy still in it?"

"Else they'd have to be very lucky."

"Jesus. Let's go down to One Man Lake and keep looking.")

William and Bullock ate the fish and sipped their coffee as the plane disappeared into the sky.

Bullock said, "So they've seen us. Now someone will come and get us. Might take a coupla hours."

At noon, Bullock said, "We've still got salt. Catch us a fish and we'll have a barbecue."

William explained what had happened to the line.

"We're fucked, then, I expect."

xi. The Last Hope

THAT DAY TWO more planes had a look at them, but none landed. William had kept the dregs of their last coffee, which he boiled up again. At dusk they knew the search was over for the day and tried to prepare themselves for another night on the island. The next morning a plane appeared early, but this time it did not bother to come down to look them over. During the day two more planes appeared, but it was clear now that they had been seen and ignored.

Bullock said suddenly, "It's the canoe. What they can see is two guys with a tent sitting in front of a fire, and a canoe fifty feet away. They reckon we're on a canoe trip. They're looking for a plane."

"Should I hide the canoe in the trees?"

"I think it's too late. They all know we're here, and they won't bother with us now, even if they notice the canoe is gone. They've told each other not to worry about the campers."

Nothing was said for some time, then Bullock continued. "William, my boy, we might be here a long time. A very long time." He looked to see if William understood him. "I'm sorry. We're finished. I should have believed that weather report."

William knew the proper response. "Nonsense. It's an accident."

Bullock looked at him thoughtfully. "I've been watching you. You've been enjoying this, so far, haven't you? Well, make it last. This is it. We're fucked now. What the hell is that!"

A few feet outside the clearing, on the lake side, a shaggy gaunt dog had appeared and was watching them. William picked up a piece of kindling and moved beside Bullock. The dog recognized the gesture and backed away.

"Wild?" William wondered.

Bullock said, "I don't know. Maybe someone abandoned it. I don't think it'll bother us."

They got through the night, and made the decision the next morning to stay where they were for one more day. "I don't know what the alternatives are, anyway," Bullock said.

Every couple of hours a plane would circle, clearly searching, before it disappeared again. William tried waving; he tried staying still; and he tried lying out flat, playing dead; but nothing excited the pilots' curiosity. That night he asked Bullock, "Is there anything to decide?"

"There might not be tomorrow morning. We can survive for a few more days without food, and Christ knows there's plenty of water, but I haven't got a lot of strength left. I *think* I need all I've got just to sit here."

At dawn, as William was making up the fire, Bullock said, "He's back. Brought his pals."

Three dogs were now watching from the edge of the trees, all the same size. Bullock said, "Now I know where they come from. They belong to Eddie Goose. He puts them on one of the islands for the summer, and comes by once in a while with a piece of meat the camp cook can't use, but mostly they look after themselves until he collects them up in the fall. Look at their ribs."

"He uses them to pull a dog-sled?"

"Eddie Goose *is* a trapper, right enough, but these look too small for that. Maybe. I don't know. But they're his dogs all right. I've seen them from the air. Had 'em pointed out by Eddie."

"Are they dangerous?"

"They might be a sign sent from God, William, my boy. Point is, I know where we are now. This is an island on Bass Lake, about four or five miles from Rice Narrows, where Eddie's band have their winter camp."

"I thought they lived across from our camp."

"Just for the summer while they're working for me, but the reservation is at Rice Narrows."

"I've fished there."

"Sure you have. But that's the limit for a day's fishing, as far as you can go and still get back to camp."

"Does it help to know where we are?"

"Sure. We just have to wait until November, then we could walk back over the ice. Make it December to be sure."

"We've got the canoe."

"We've got a guy with a broken arm, a canoe without a paddle, and ten miles to go with two portages. We haven't eaten for two days and not much before that. What are our chances?"

William considered. "I would say we've reached the point where we go now or not at all. I can still get us into the canoe, I think, and paddle a bit so that we can follow the current. The longer we stay here the weaker I'll get."

"Then let's go."

An hour later William had plugged the hole in the canoe with a piece of stick wrapped in the torn-off cuff of his shirt.

He made Bullock as comfortable as he could in the front of the canoe, and pushed off across the lake, south. They took with them a saucepan for a water vessel, the groundsheet, and the plywood top of the lunch-box split in half to use as paddles.

For directions, they knew that all the water in the area flowed south, passing the Loon Lake camp on its way to join another system. They knew, too, that after four or five miles they should see some sign of Rice Narrows, and perhaps start to recognize the country.

He paddled all afternoon, holding the top and one side of the piece of plywood. His gloves and hat were still in the plane, so he tore two strips off his shirt-sleeves to wrap around his palms, but every time he looked down, the wooden edge had worked its way past the cloth and was digging into his skin. By late afternoon there was a deep open wound across each palm, and he tried to make a pad of the blood-soaked bits of cloth and hold the paddle with his fingers. The canoe was barely moving. Bullock croaked something from under his groundsheet, and William leaned down to hear.

"You're burning up," Bullock said.

William became conscious then of what he had been feeling for some time. For as long as the sun had been out it had been beating down on the part of his head normally protected by his cap, and now he was in danger of sunstroke, or a bad burn. There wasn't much he could do about it. He poured some water over his head with the saucepan, and after that, whenever he felt the sun, he wetted his head, but he knew that if he could feel it, he was probably late.

They came to their first portage, an easy one at other times, but getting Bullock out and over the rocky hump to the launching place on the other side of the neck of land took most of his remaining strength, and he couldn't lift the canoe, just drag it the two hundred feet to the other side.

Bullock said, "Let's stop for the night. Maybe a rest will help. Your hands hurt?"

"Yes, they do."

"We need a fire to get through the night."

"I'll make one in a minute."

It was much easier this time. The sun had already done a good job of drying out enough kindling, so that assembling fuel was simple, and the fire lit with a single match.

When he had it roaring, he said to Bullock, "We've still got three matches."

"It's a triumph, that's what it is."

As the night progressed, the pain in his hands grew more and more intense, and he gave up trying to sleep, concentrating on keeping the fire going.

At some point in the small hours, Bullock said, "Can you sing?"

"No."

"Okay, then. I'll tell you the story of my life, and then you tell me yours. I think we should try to stay awake." And he did, not from the beginning, but from the time he took his gratuity when he returned from the war in Europe and bought a Norseman, intending never again to have a boss, and when he saw this area from above, decided how he wanted to spend the rest of his life; how he'd found a backer for the first few buildings and then a bank wanted to lend him some to expand, but then, in a way, the bank would be his boss, so he canvassed the guys who'd fished there already and got enough backing from them to build the new buildings; and then he'd bought a second plane, then a third and a fourth, and now he was thinking of opening up farther north, a camp specializing in arctic char.

Even in his condition, able only to croak quietly, he was a good talker, shaping the stories well. "Your turn," he said, when he was done.

William had some difficulty finding anything worth retelling. He had gone to school, then university, come to Canada as a student, become a teacher, been fired, then caught a bus to where he had met Bullock on the town dock, and here he was. But Bullock poked at him, monosyllabically, until William revealed that his present situation could be traced back to the stories he had read as a child, ridiculous stories of Indians and Mounties and trappers in canoes.

"And here you are. Just like in the stories."

"Here I am."

"And here *I* am, saved by William the Moody, the boy guide. Or so far saved. What next?"

"We keep paddling as long as I can."

"I mean you. Suppose we get out of this. What are you going to do?"

"I was thinking about that before we left. Having been a guide will give me some rights here. Do you know what I mean? I'm not an absolute outsider any more. More like a resident alien. But I'm a teacher by trade, and a student by vocation. I want to go back to school."

"I think you've got more rights than that. When will you start school, if we get out of here?"

"As soon as I've got enough money. And it's very late to apply so I might have to wait another year, but that's where I belong."

"You could work for me. I need an assistant manager."

"No. No more administration. I want to read, now."

"Just read? Nothing else? Eat steak? Drink whisky? Get laid? See some movies?"

"Oh, yes. All of those things. But most of all I want to read."

The sun was above the horizon. William dipped some water from the lake and they drank and wetted their heads, and struck camp. It was impossible to grip the piece of plywood without reopening the wounds in his hands. William attached the wood to his forearm with his trouser belt and moved it by pulling and pushing with his closed fist. Unrolling his hands after a night's inactivity was also impossible and would have to be someone else's problem, someone in a hospital. With the plywood tied to his arm, he was able to keep the canoe point-ed in the right direction, and even generate a tiny forward motion. All morning they edged along the shore. Once a plane passed, and William waved, and got an answering wig-wag.

("They aren't making very good time. Where do you think they're headed for?"

"I doubt if they know themselves. Look at that asshole in the front with the groundsheet over his head. That's not a serious canoeist."

"Let's make one more circle here then go and have supper. Hang on. What the fuck is that?"

"What?"

"That shadow, under the surface. Look, I'll turn around and come in at the same angle. Now! Look, look, you see it?"

"Holy Christ. It's the plane. They must have gone straight down."

"They wouldn't have stood a chance. Let's get back and get some divers up here."

"How come those canoeists didn't see it?"

"It's the angle. The way the light hits the water. Like you can see reefs better from up here.")

xii. Saved

AT NOON THEY came to another portage. William got Bullock out of the canoe and propped against a tree, and wondered if he would be able to get him across the portage. Bullock was unable to help himself.

The portage was about a hundred feet long, a rocky slope with only a very slight rise and a similar shallow descent down to the other shore. Under ordinary circumstances, a very easy portage. William got Bullock on to his feet and shuffled forward foot by foot to the top. Going up took strength, but going down to the shore was harder because of the difficulty of keeping Bullock from toppling. William got him to the shore, finally, and sat him down with his back against a large rock. He returned and dragged the canoe to the top of the slope, then, trying to get his wrist hooked over the side of the canoe without hurting his hand, lost control. The canoe slid away from him, too fast to catch, but slowly enough so that it would not do itself any damage. Then William could see what might happen at the bottom and he tried to cry out, but, before he could get his mouth working, the prow of the canoe had caught Bullock in the shoulder and sent him sprawling face forward on the rock, where he lay with his already-broken arm under him until William could get to him.

He turned him over gently and poured some water on his face and Bullock opened his eyes. There was no need for him to explain. One of the splints was sticking out free and the angle of his arm showed that the other hadn't been enough to protect him.

It seemed to William that the next manoeuvre would be the last he would be able to manage. After that, the gods could do what they liked. He dragged Bullock into the canoe, toppling him carefully over the side so that he fell on his good arm, and pushed off. He threw some water over the camp owner and got a flicker of response, which gave him a shot of hope, like hearing a cough from a long-unresponsive starting motor, and he sank the plywood paddle into the water.

Two hours later, he knew he should be wetting his head because he kept emerging into consciousness from some other realm. He thought the visions would come soon, remembering what they might resemble, from the third man (hooded) who would appear in the canoe, to God's boots; perhaps voices, even: "Had enough, William?" And then, across the lake he saw a white shape, a boat, going slowly along the shoreline, and he saw that he knew this shoreline, and the lake itself, and he was back in the place he had been lost on the first day's guiding, back in a familiar neighbourhood after crossing the watery desert, and this boat was real, one of Bullock's. He moistened his lips to try for a sound, a single shout, knowing that more than one would not be there, and only trying at all because of the way sound carries across water. When he was ready he knelt in the canoe, his stomach braced against the thwart, and croaked loudly once and waved the plywood paddle. Then he collapsed in the bottom of the canoe and waited, not for long, for the sound of the outboard motor as it raced across the lake towards them.

Seated in the prow, a towel over his head like a burnous, held in place with a piece of string, was R. Brown. "I've been looking for you," he said. "Don't get up. Arnold and I will tow you back."

Two days later, Bullock, after consulting with R. Brown, sent for Billy Vernon, the local Member of the Provincial Parliament and Minister for Colleges and Universities, to attend him in hospital. Bullock was the largest contributor of campaign funds in Vernon's ledger. He had tried to get Bullock to accept a variety of patronage appointments, but Bullock's only motive in contributing the money was to make sure that he would know in advance of any legislation that might affect his business, and Vernon and his party remained heavily in Bullock's debt. Now Bullock explained exactly what he wanted to know and to know immediately, and when Vernon reported back the same day, Bullock told him what he wanted done. When Vernon protested he could not interfere with a body that must stay at arm's length from the government, Bullock told him to try.

First Vernon telephoned his own deputy minister to get started on the difficult part of Bullock's request, then he called the president of Van Horne, who in turn called Bone Bishop, member of the board of governors of Van Horne, and vice-president of Simcoe University.

At Bullock's insistence, William spent a week convalescing as Bullock's guest at the camp. Bullock flew a nurse in twice a day to dress his hands, and treat the badly sunburned area of his head. "At least you won't look like a farmer any more," the nurse said. William looked at himself in the mirror she held up, wondering what she was talking about, and saw that the line that used to run across his forehead that marked the edge of his cap was gone. In its place was a welt of red-and-brown blisters that reached up into his hair. That night, R. Brown brought him the front page of the weekly paper. There was a picture of William in bed, his hands bandaged. The caption was, "Local Guide's Knowledge of Bush Saves Camp-Owner's Life."

Near the end of the week he received a letter from the Council for the Arts, telling him that a candidate had been unable to take up his grant and therefore they were offering it to the next qualified person, who was William. "Too late, though," he explained to Bullock. "I wouldn't get accepted in the university now."

"Try," Bullock said. "Here, let's send them a telegram. Tell me what to say."

William dictated a formal message, which Bullock relayed, less formally, to Billy Vernon, who called Bone Bishop, and the next morning William had his acceptance. His happiness was completed when he received a letter from Gloria, telling him that she was returning to Simcoe to do a degree in Library Science.

He had one thing left to do, one decision to make. R. Brown attended him during his convalescence, playing gin rummy and bringing him the beer and chocolate he craved. Before he left he asked Brown whether it would be kinder to give Arnold Banting the half-gallon of whisky in his bag, now under his bed, or quietly (for Arnold's sake) pour it down the toilet. It was not a thing he wanted to carry around with him. Finally the two men decided it would be irresponsible to give the whisky to Arnold. They agreed that William should give a sort of party with it on his last night, sharing the bottle with all the guides. It would work out to about two medium-sized drinks each. But when William went to get the whisky from his bag, the bottle was empty.

EPILOGUE

TWO YEARS LATER, William was in his study, preparing for the doctoral examinations he was to begin writing a week later. He had abandoned the Romantics. His experience at Loon Lake had made him curious about other and similar experiences, and he had decided to explore his new interest and capitalize on it by switching to Canadian Studies. He made the move for proper reasons, but it was politically sound as well, for these were early days in Canadian Studies. Compared with the Romantics, there was very little to know about Canadian literature, and few who cared. In fact, there had been objections to allowing William his thesis: "Fiction and Fact in the Narratives of the Early Settlers." But the objections were based in ignorance and snobbishness, and the objectors lost their nerve in the face of the new nationalism that was stirring: the thesis was allowed to stand.

William was worried about the Old English paper, and he was counting on *Beowulf* to get him through. He got a lot of help from Geoffrey Spindle. "Who would have thought that anyone would want to know Anglo-Saxon again, eh?" he said, when William asked him to tutor him. "A recovery of the old learning."

There was a knock at the door. R. Brown poked his head round. "May I come in, sir?"

"It still isn't necessary for you to call me 'sir.' We're both students here together."

"To me you will always be 'sir,' sir. What are you doing?"

"*Beowulf.* For the generals."

"What's it like? Should I take the course in fourth year?"

"This is very hard work. Leave me alone so I can get on with it."

"All right. I must do the rounds anyway." R. Brown owned three automobile repair shops, which he had set up with a government Youth Loan. The income from these shops kept him in comfort while he studied English literature at Simcoe. "Do you ever wonder what would have happened if you had got the job of president, sir?" he asked as he was leaving.

"Yes. I would have been very unhappy. I wouldn't have had any time to read. Now go away and let me work."

There was one more conversation before the generals. On a day in March, Mordecai came to see him. William had almost forgotten him, but he was immediately interested again in his old colleague's progress. The redonning of the blue blazer and grey trousers suggested clearly that he had moved on.

"Goodbye golden youth?" William asked.

"What? Oh, yes. Long, long ago. Tell you the truth, I am once again a non-contender, no longer interested. Too old."

"In terms of Cockayne's Syndrome, you mean. You look the same."

"Yes. In those terms I am about seventy-five."

"Well, so much for that, eh?"

"Not quite. You see, I enjoy company now, especially the company of women, most of all a former colleague of ours. Remember Maisie? *I* don't care about the sex thing, but you can't expect everybody else to be the same way. She doesn't care much, either, but, looking ahead, she adores children. So one has obligations."

"I'm sorry."

"Don't bleed for me, old boy. I manage. I've got this needle I stick in it once a week. It's good for an hour. Does the job. Well, I must be off. Shall you come back to Van Horne when you're a doctor?"

"First things first. Let me get Grendel's mother out of the way. By the way, whatever happened to Jane Goray?"

"Disappeared in a puff of smoke. She took Clem Stokes's job up at the Ministry and when the premier amalgamated all the ministries responsible for education they had too many civil servants. She was still waiting to be made permanent, so they made her redundant instead. No one has seen her since."

"When did that happen?"

"Shortly after she arrived at the Buildings."

Mordecai left. William sucked his pencil. The great trick with translation was to find a word with the right meaning but as different a sound as possible. "Aglaecwif," for example. Not "ugly-wife," surely. "Monstrous woman"?

He looked at his watch. Gloria had promised to come by soon, and they would go for a walk across the campus to a coffee-shop where they would sit looking at each other for an hour. As soon as he knew the results of his exams, they were going to marry. But there was a lot to do before then.

POSTSCRIPT

THE CEREMONY WAS almost over. The magazine columnist had been given his honorary degree for his
contribution to education, and made a very long speech about
the importance of magazines to Canadian culture. The graduates had received their degrees and now were listening to the
farewell address from the president. William paid no attention. Not that the president's speech was dull. R. Brown could
be trusted to send the graduates into the world with style and
wit. He delivered the same speech to all of the convocations
and it bore repetition. But William knew it well and he abandoned himself to the luxury of wool-gathering. Thirty years
before, Cunningham had stood where R. Brown was now,
delivering his version of the same speech. R. Brown himself
had received his certificate in Automobile Engineering the year
after, following it, as soon as he had made some money, with
a degree in English, a master's degree in philosophy, and a doctorate in the classics.

William looked around the stage and noted the absences.
Mordecai was alive but retired, a bright-eyed old man whose
whole delight lay in his six children and his score of grandchildren. Bodger had gone to his rest, and so had Geoffrey
Spindle.

Some of his colleagues, whom William thought of as "the new people," had been there for twenty years, and had stopped talking about the need to get new blood into the department. When William was awarded his doctorate, he had considered the positions offered to him across Canada, and concluded that Van Horne was still the most attractive choice. The chairman, who had been among the first people William had hired, was pleased to have him back, but his hope of teaching his new subject was doomed. When he expressed the wish, Canadian Studies were just beginning to boom, and before long it was possible to major in literature in some universities without bothering with the literary history of other countries — Elizabethan England, for example — but to concentrate entirely, at least up to the Master's level, on Canadiana, so there were plenty of courses to be taught. But, at the same time, the voices that urged the expansion of Canlit also urged that foreigners not be allowed to teach it on the grounds that — but William was never sure what the grounds were. It was enough that the accent which had served him so well in the bush barred him from his specialty, then and later. Instead, he was eventually given a half-course in the English Romantics, and on the whole he was glad. The people teaching Canlit consulted him regularly, and he never got tired of the subject, producing little essays on nineteenth-century pioneer literature from time to time for Canadian periodicals and even giving two radio talks on the CBC. He *was* especially interested in primitive or folk literature: the letters, the stories in parish magazines (he collected lay sermons in manuscript), and the memoirs people wrote of their families to leave to their children.

He had a wife (Gloria) who loved him, a son whom he had taught to fish, and a daughter who still wanted him to play tennis with her, and he was respected in the classroom. From the outside, and from time to time on the inside, too, he was a happy man.

R. Brown came to his conclusion, was applauded, and the assembly rose to sing "O Canada." William always enjoyed the anthem, having gone to the trouble, when he came back from Loon Lake, to learn all the words both in English and French, to express to himself how he felt.

There followed the processional down the auditorium out on to the sunlit grass of the quadrangle. Two or three of his students sought to introduce him to their parents; he drank a cup of tea with the magazine columnist; and then he was free. He looked at his watch. In two hours he would be on a plane. He would be met and taken to a lake where a bush plane would fly him to Loon Lake, to spend a week fishing with a white-haired Harry Bullock. As part of the ritual, on his last day there, Bullock would fly the two of them up to Bass Lake, the place where if you came in at the right angle you could still see the wreck of the Norseman beneath the surface. They never landed. They looked, and Bullock flew back to camp along the route William had tried to paddle, and William came back to town.

He had told no one the whole story, not even his son, who had wondered how he got to be such an expert fisherman. Instead, he planned to write it as part of a longer memoir in the tradition of the literature he was studying. So far he had reached the point of his arrival in Canada. It would be another year, probably, before he got to Loon Lake, but he did not repine. Almost every month in proper academic fashion he added a little note of something he had just remembered or realized, a note against the day when he would begin.

Sept. 9-95.